Hit the Road Jack

Frank English

2QT Limited (Publishing)

First Edition published 2017

2QT Limited (Publishing)
Unit 5 Commercial Courtyard
Duke Street
Settle
North Yorkshire
BD24 9RH

Copyright © Frank English 2017
The right of Frank English to be identified as the author of this work has been asserted by him in accordance with the Copyright, Designs and Patents Act 1988

All rights reserved. This book is sold subject to the condition that no part of this book is to be reproduced, in any shape or form. Or by way of trade, stored in a retrieval system or transmitted in any form or by any means, electronic, mechanical, photocopying, recording, be lent, re-sold, hired out or otherwise circulated in any form of binding or cover other than that in which it is published and without a similar condition, including this condition being imposed on the subsequent purchaser, without prior permission of the copyright holder

Cover design: Charlotte Mouncey
Cover images: main photographs supplied by ©Frank English
Additional images from iStockhoto.com

Printed in the UK by Lightning Source UK Limited

ISBN 978-1-912014-51-4

To John

To mi Mam, Florence May English.
Always in mind.

with best wishes

Frank Gopher

To John

Chapter 1

"Who the bloody 'ell's that, at this time of day?" Jud muttered, at the incessantly impatient rattling of the side door.

"Then why doesn't thy go and have a look," Marion answered sharply, "and stop being so bloomin' grumpy?"

"I've onny just started mi cup of tea, for goodness' sake," he grumbled.

"It's Marion that'll be answering the door, then?" she replied sarcastically. "I'll put *my* tea down and go and have a look, shall I?"

"Sarky bugger," Jud muttered, as she opened the inner door on to the small porch.

"You took your time," her visitor quipped with a grin.

"Jack!" she exclaimed with a note of excitement dispelling her mood. "Our Jack. My, it's good to see a friendly face and hear a cheerful voice, for once. Come in, lad, come in. Why is it you always seem to know when a fresh pot has been mashed?"

"Knack? Skill?" he suggested, as he took off his shoes in the porch. "Or is it that there's *always* one on the go, any time of day or night?"

He hugged and kissed her like he'd not seen her for an eternity.

"Mi granddad not in, then?" he added, noticing that he wasn't sitting in his favourite arm chair by the hearth.

"He's in t'front room, love," she answered, dropping to a whisper, almost. "Not been too well lately. His chest's playing him up."

"Mmm," Jack muttered, concerned to hear that. "Doctor been?"

"He has that," she said. "Says there might be summat up wi' his gall bladder, as well, whatever that is."

"I'm sorry to hear that," Jack replied, sipping his tea. "Gall bladder?"

"Aye, lad," a deep voice joined them from the front room doorway. "Thinks it might be gall stones."

"Granddad," Jack shouted, leaping to his feet to hug the big man.

"Steady on, Our Jack," Jud warned. "Just a bit ... delicate at the moment, si thi."

"Oh aye, Owd Cock?" Jack puzzled, backing off a bit. "I'm rayt sorry to 'ear that."

"Yon lass o' thine bearin' up all rayt?" Jud asked, a grin growing in his face the first time for some weeks. "Sent thee aht for a bit o' peace, eh?"

"Summat like that," Jack laughed. "I just wanted to come and spend a bit of time with you during mi holidays, you know. Don't get much time when I'm in school."

"But you were onny here in May last," Marion puzzled. "Whitsuntide, wasn't it? And now it's end of August. Everything all right with yon ... Lee, wasn't it? How long have you been together now?"

Jack was quiet for a moment or two as he drank his tea and nibbled on a digestive in front of the fire.

"Been married for just over twelve months," he said slowly, staring into the flames, "and everything's all right, I suppose. It's just that – living in the same house as her dad – she seems to want to spend more time with him than me."

"Do you think it might be because she feels sorry for

him?" Marion asked, trying to find a meaning to it all. "I mean, he *is* on his own, and she *is* his daughter."

"You all right, Grandma?" Jack asked, a smile creeping up on him. "It's not like you to give anybody the benefit of the doubt."

"Cheeky young bugger," she harrumphed with a grin. "There's got to be *some* reason, hasn't there?"

Marion was no fool. She knew instinctively things weren't right. Hadn't she known Jack's ways and strangenesses almost as well as his mam for all the years she had known him? Because he didn't show his feelings that often, he found it hard to hide entirely what was important to him. It would come out, she was sure, when he was good and ready, and not a moment sooner.

"How long you stopping, then?" Jud asked, as he sat down in his favourite kitchen chair.

"Well," Jack started, choosing his words carefully so as not to worry them, "Lee has the car – her car – so I'm on the train. I was wondering if I might stay over a couple of nights? Get chance a to catch up, really."

"Of course you can, love," Marion said, glancing across at her husband. "Stay as long as you like."

-o-

"That was a lovely tea, Grandma," Jack smiled, pushing his empty plate away. "One of my all-time favourites."

"It was only egg, bacon, and beans," she said, a puzzled frown on her face. "Don't you get anything better at home?"

"Doesn't matter what I get, Grandma," Jack said calmly, "as long as I like it. Lee doesn't usually try to give me stuff I won't eat."

"Aye, Our Jack," his granddad laughed, "tha allus were definite about what tha would and wouldn't ayt for thi dinner."

"None of yon tripe or liver or kidneys," Jack insisted

with a grimace and a shudder. "That's an offal dinner."

They all laughed as they settled by the glowing fire. Jack was back and at home, the stresses of everyday living melting away and taking him back to when he was a nipper again. He was concerned about his granddad's health, though, but it wouldn't do to labour it *too* much. Although Jud would expect him to be concerned, because it wouldn't be Jack if he wasn't, he wouldn't expect him to cause a fuss. What he had he couldn't change, like hordes of coal miners before him, and countless ones after, no doubt.

"Shall we be allotmenting tomorrow then, Granddad?" Jack asked, looking forward to seeing their old stomping ground. He was quite staggered to think it was nigh on twenty years since that first time he had smelled Tommy Stoke's pig muck, and had seen Tom Smith's duck shed. These memories brought fond feelings back to his mind, and a dimpled smile to his face.

"'Fraid not, Our Jack," Jud said sadly. "Had to give up the second one a month or so ago. Couldn't cope wi' it any more, tha knows."

"But what about yon greenhouses," Jack sighed, "and all those memories we shared there?"

"Got a good price for the greenhouses," Jud said, putting a brave face on it all, "but memories can't be priced or sold. Anyway, *they* stay in mi heart and mi head. They'll be wi' me as long as iver I'm 'ere. Be rayt."

"I'm sorry to hear that, Owd Cock," Jack said quietly and with a good deal of sorrow; sorrow which he would never let his granddad see. "Tha taught me all I know about all sorts of stuff up yonder, and I know it won't amount to much in t'grand scheme of things, but it'll allus stay wi' me, tha knows."

The room fell silent as insistent, crepuscular night sneaked in under doors and around curtains, challenging the crackling fire to fight its onslaught.

"'As tha been to see thi mam's grave yet, Our Jack?" Jud asked as he drew the curtains and switched on the table lamp.

"Not this time, Granddad," Jack replied. "Not yet. Now that we won't be allotmenting tomorrow, I thought I'd pay her a visit, and tidy things up with some fresh flowers. Not the same from Womack's florist, though, I don't think. Not the same as yours…"

They drifted into an uneasy silence as they watched the shiny black nuggets spitting and hissing in the fire grate. Black diamonds, he called them, as each man struggled with his own personal fears for the future. Jack's thoughts of his mam were hijacked by Lee constantly, as if she were telling him he ought to come back to her – soon.

He felt like he didn't belong there any more, with the space for him in *her* life lessening as their lives moved on. He didn't begrudge the time she spent with her dad, or the fact that they were living in *his* house. Ron had prevailed upon her to let him buy the house, which she would inherit when he died. Jack had never felt comfortable with this. His wife seemed happy with the arrangement, so he let it slide.

True to his principles and feelings of propriety, disquiet began to grow, which he shared with her. Quarrels had started to surface and increase, usually out of nothing much, but they left increasingly indelible residues in his mind. This sort of thing shouldn't have been happening, but he didn't have anyone impartial with whom he might share his disquiet.

-o-

"Well, mi owd love," he muttered at his mam's graveside as he weeded and titivated her garden, "I wish you were here to talk to. You were allus there to smooth troubled pathways, weren't you? Now things are getting beyond my control and understanding. I miss you. I miss you a lot."

"Jack?" a quietly surprised little voice urged him to notice its presence. His conscious thoughts resurfaced to a very real and painfully familiar face.

"Jenny?" he gasped, his eyes focusing on the one woman who could cause him pain and take it away at the same time. "What are *you* doing here?"

"I could say the same about you," she laughed nervously. "Of all the people in the world, of all the places, I should have known I might see you here."

"Then…?" he puzzled.

"My dad," she said, tears springing to her eyes, as her voice dropped to a hoarse whisper. "Heart attack two months ago."

"Oh, Jenny," he said putting his arms around her and drawing her close. "I'm so sorry."

She sighed deeply, and her body relaxed as he drew her even closer.

"You've no idea how I've longed for that feeling of closeness to you," she whispered.

"Oh, yes, I have," he replied. "I've thought about you all the time since that horrible day I deserted you when you needed me most. I shouldn't have left you like that. I should have been there for you. Friends Forever? Remember? We had a pact, and I let you down."

"It was all you could have done," she said, "and I don't blame you. I was the one who let *you* down, and now—"

"Both married to someone else," he sighed, "when it should have been us together forever."

"You? Married?" Jenny's disbelieving voice betraying her emotion.

"Yes," he said quietly, "to someone I thought I loved, but—"

"Not as much as you thought you might?" she added.

"Ever the intuitive," he smiled. "You always could see

into my soul, Jenny McDermot."

"Not well enough, Jack Ingles," she replied, a note of bitter self-recrimination creeping into her voice. "Had I been able to do that successfully, things would perhaps have been ... different."

"Not your fault," he continued. "I kept my feelings hidden, even from you, because I was afraid of where they might take me – afraid of having deeper feelings for my friend, and I've suffered for it ever since."

"Oh, Jack," she sighed, holding him tighter. "If only..."

"We can't do this," he gasped, stepping back from their clinch. "We're both married, and need ... should ... ought to go..."

"We don't live together anymore," her whispered words crept from her lips.

"B–b–but...?" he stammered, a brief frown of uncertainty beginning to dance around his brows.

"It was a huge mistake," she explained. "First the baby, and then agreeing to a sham marriage to give my daughter a father. If I hadn't agreed out of blind panic, you and I—"

"Would have been together," he interrupted, revelling in the thought that he would have found peace and comfort at last.

"I can't, Jenny," he went on. "I've always loved you. I admitted it to myself finally when you told me, and that had been the problem all along, accepting that *you* were the one I should have been with."

"I know," she said, taking hold of his hand and kissing it tenderly.

"But," he continued, "I have to try to make my marriage work. I owe Lee that much, at least."

Taking hold of her gently and drawing her unresisting body to him, he met her responsive lips in a passionate kiss, pouring all his love and tenderness into her as he had never kissed a woman before. She sighed desperately as she held him more tightly, not wanting to let go … as if her life depended upon it.

They parted finally, both drawing air greedily into their near-bursting lungs.

"We *will* meet again, Jenny McDermot," he promised, a look of hope in his eyes, trying to dispel the anguish and despair he felt in his heart. "I don't know when, but I promise that if you love me, you will give me a chance to prove to you that all this should have happened sooner."

"I will always love you, Jack," she promised, "and this time I *will* wait. My daughter, Jessie, will love you too. Promise."

They walked to the cemetery gates hand in hand, not able to believe that this wasn't a dream. They turned their separate ways along Church Lane, not daring to cast a backward glance.

"18 Queen Street," a little voice floated back once he had reached Firville Avenue, "if you care to visit at any time."

Then she was gone.

His maelstrom of feelings washed him about from one extreme to another, past the Grammar School sports field on Dalefield Road – where he had enjoyed much athletic success as a boy – over the beck by the Huntsman Pub, and on to his grandma's estate. Jenny had forced an entirely new set of emotions to the surface – emotions he thought he had buried. Raw, painful and … exciting. How could he feel like this? What should have been! What should he do?

-o-

As usual, the diesel train journey back to Leeds gave him time to reflect on what had just happened to him, and on how he was going to handle the future. He was on his way back to the woman he had married and whom he thought he loved. The woman he should have married wanted him to stay and take up the life they should have enjoyed a long time before. In Jack's way of thinking, life wasn't meant to be so complicated. He had always been a complicatedly simple soul who wouldn't have chosen to be drawn into such a complex pattern of relationships. If only things had been sorted out before he had finished college…

The couple of days he had spent with his grandparents just relaxing and enjoying their company had been wonderful. His granddad had always enjoyed the simple pleasures of their being together, but his grandma wasn't so simple or gullible. She knew why he had come. Marion was nobody's fool.

His granddad's condition worried him. He had noticed a marked and significant deterioration in not only how he *was* physically, but on how he *viewed* himself. It was almost as if he knew what was around the corner, and was wanting to meet it head on – dour, pragmatic owd Yorkshireman that he was.

"Waste o' time tryin' to prevent t'inevitable," he always would say.

-o-

The slag heaps from Pope and Peardson's colliery near Altofts station drew the three carriage chuggy diesel train to a slow mid-platform stop. Two people got off and one person got on – a young lady with a pushchair, but nothing to push in it.

"Strange," Jack thought, but his present dilemma soon ushered it to the back of his mind.

Of even greater concern than his granddad's condition was the speed and ease with which he had embraced the love of his life. Jenny wasn't a passing phase, a whim. She had always lived in the 'what if?' part of his mind, and they had always shared everything. Would he share his reawakening feelings for her with his wife? He didn't think so. This would be his secret. Secret? From Lee? What had things come to?

Early evening on Sunday was never a busy time on this line, particularly during school holidays. There always seemed to be delays because of line repairs, signal failures, or slow turnaround times at the stations en route. This train pulled into each, picking up few passengers, but an inordinate amount of freight, to be dropped off at one stop or other along the line. Consequently, it allowed Jack a lot of figuring out time, and the chance to count the exact number of fields given over to rhubarb cultivation in the Triangle around Methley – a crop which kept the country going during the war years just past.

The sprawl of the Yorkshire Copper Works at Stourton and its hidden processes never ceased to amaze and intrigue Jack, if only as an outer sentinel of the approach to Hunslet Junction, and the long slow Holbeck curve into Leeds City station itself. Jack had travelled this line so many times during his college years that he knew instinctively where he was by the alarming judder and sway of his carriage over the points, and the protesting screech of rigid steel wheels being coerced around gently curving and equally unyielding steel tracks.

Leeds City station drew him home, finally allowing him to tread terra firma and to reclaim his bearings once again. He was glad to be back in what he now considered to be his home town – glad that he no longer had to endure these seemingly endlessly jolted journeys. Yet he was sad at the passing of the excitement and danger of riding his Fire Dragons into battle.

He wasn't looking forward to his homecoming at all. He had left on a sour note, and now he wasn't sure what sort of a greeting he would meet. The relations between Jack and his wife had been strained lately, to say the least, and they spent little time in each other's company. She had taken to sleeping in the spare room out of choice, and had been spending more time with her dad. This wasn't what Jack had signed up for – and it took him back to his childhood where household tensions had become a way of life.

"Hello Lee," he shouted as he opened the front door tentatively. "I'm back."

A light hand took hold of his arm from behind, spun him round, and – pressing warm and moist lips next to his – drew herself to him in a passionate hug. He hadn't expected such a greeting from his wife.

"I'm glad you're back," she whispered. "I've missed you, and … Dad's out until later. So…"

She broke off, and taking his hand in both hers, she drew him towards the stairs, a smile on her face and desire in her eyes.

Chapter 2

Jenny sat in her front room, nursing her daughter, a faraway look in her face and tears in her eyes. She had never expected to meet Jack like that, nor to have her emotions shredded – again. Yet, they *had* met, and he *had* vowed his love for her. That had to mean something, didn't it? She would wait. She had promised. But when would she see him again? When would he become part of her life again? When would he become *her* Jack, like it had always been? When would she experience that gut-wrenching and emotional earthquake she had felt in his arms in the churchyard?

"Jack," she sighed as she nursed her bairn. "Oh, Jack."

Jenny's dad might have been a boorishly overbearing man at times, but he had provided well for his family, including Jenny and her daughter, Jessie. He had doted on *her* little girl just like he had *his*. He had loved his younger daughter with a passion that threw an impenetrable screen around her, keeping outsiders where they belonged. Unlike her sister, Jenny knew how to manipulate her dad, understanding from a very early age which finger she was able to wind him around. Consequently, she had a great deal more latitude in her relationship with him than had her sister.

She loved her dad, and had taken his passing very hard. With him around she would have endured and overcome the hardships of bringing up a child on her own. Mum had wanted them to stay with her at home, where there was plenty of space and all the help she could possibly need. Unfortunately, although her mum undoubtedly meant well and desperately wanted to help, she made it quite clear from the outset that *she* knew better how to raise a child. Jenny couldn't live with this, and so took the only way out – number 18 Queen Street ... and independence.

Jenny's husband had turned out to be a ne'er-do-well as her dad had predicted, making it abundantly clear that he wanted nothing to do with nappies and disturbed sleep. Consequently, he had voted with his feet a month before Jessie's arrival, leaving no forwarding address.

Her dad had left enough provision in his will for her to be able to manage without having to work, but this was only a stop gap until Jessie was old enough for school. Jenny didn't see herself as a stop-at-home mum for the rest of her life. There would be time in the next year or two to put the first-class honours degree she had managed to complete before Jessie was born to good use, and to stretch her mind ... and her wings.

All that was before Jack stepped back over her horizon, allowing her to hope again by rekindling what she felt she was meant to be – Mrs Jenny Ingles. She dare not think, dare not hope, but he ... had promised he would be back ... one day. She believed him, her Jack. He never broke a promise, so she had every faith in him that he would return.

Dare she look that far ahead? He was married, for God's sake. Was he happily married, though? But he had kissed her passionately and held he desperately close. Was that the action of a happily married man in love with his wife? The last time Jenny had felt such passion, such core-shaking emotion, was in the café as he had held her hands. Then, as now, a lightning charge had ripped through her body, setting every nerve, every feeling on edge. This was more than she could cope with – more than she could have hoped for. She wanted him. With all her being, she wanted him – now.

"Jenny," a clear, familiar voice rang out from the front door, bursting in to her cocoon and dissipating her dreams. "You in, love?"

"In here," she called back, clearing her throat, trying desperately to hide the raw emotions her mother might otherwise detect. She needed to draw a veil of perceived normality she wouldn't be able to peer through.

"Been to your dad's grave?" she asked. "Only ... I have some chrysanths I wanted taking."

"Just had a walk with Jessie," she assured her, "to tidy it up a bit."

"See anybody?" her mum asked, a frown crossing her brow.

"One or two folks," Jenny added. "You know. Just ... folks."

"Then who was the man you were seen kissing?" her mother asked pointedly.

"Your secret police force out again, eh, Mum?" her daughter countered. "Mrs Davis on Dalefield Avenue, or Mrs Ivers behind the cemetery? Hmm?"

"Well?" her mother insisted.

"Just an old friend, for goodness' sake," Jenny replied, irritated that she was sticking her nose into her business as usual.

"Then he must have been a very good 'old' friend," Mum harrumphed indignantly, "to have had you in such a close clinch."

"Mother," Jenny said quietly, turning to face her antagonist, "I'll say this only once. Call off your rude and nosey cronies, and mind – your – own – bloody – business."

"I'm only trying—" she protested.

"To run my life, as usual," Jenny burst in again, eyes

flashing. "So, keep out, stop spying, or we're moving, and then see what you'll do without seeing your granddaughter."

"Haven't you some shopping you said needed doing, Mum?" another familiar voice joined the gathering.

"Val?" Jenny's said through a shaking voice. "Is that really you? But how…?"

Jenny's sister closed the outside door, strode into the room, and drew her close.

"It's been a while, Sis," she said, almost apologetically, "but you know only too well how it is with children. How is my gorgeous little niece?"

"I'll get off, then," their mother interrupted. "I'll see you later, Val, and you too, Jenny, if I'm allowed back in."

"For goodness' sake get over yourself, Mum," Jenny replied, a sardonic smile growing around her mouth. "I'm a grown woman, and I *can* look after myself."

"Coffee and one of those gorgeous scones you seem to magic out of thin air?" Val smiled. "I could never get the hang. You really must show me … one of these days."

"To what do I owe the honour of this visit, O sister mine?" Jenny said, once mother had left the building. "Royal summons?"

"Actually, no," Val replied as her sister poured the coffee. "I felt it was time we spent a few days together. William is looking after the children, school's out, so here I am. How are you, and, more to the point, how's little Jessie?"

"We're OK, really," Jenny replied, "as long as folks keep their noses out of our business and leave us alone."

"She's only looking out for you, you know," Val said, trying to tread that delicate placatory line between mother and younger daughter. "Since Dad died, she feels she's been very much backed into a corner with your situation, and—"

"Hang on a bit," Jenny butted in. "I thought this was about me and Jessie. 'Time we spent a few days together'. Remember?"

"I can't just ignore Mum's worries and concerns," Val replied, somewhat on the defensive, knowing how sharp her little sister could be.

"Fine way she has of showing it," Jenny snapped.

"Can we just get this – whatever it is – out of the way?" Val asked, a pleading tone hanging in the air between them. "Then we can enjoy being together? For a while, at least."

"All right," Jenny agreed reluctantly, "but be quick."

"Mum reckons you've been seen in a passionate clinch with some good-looking man," Val started slowly, not really feeling right with all of this. "I know it's none of my concern, but is it true?"

"You are right," he sister answered. "It *is* none of your concern … and that's the way it will stay. I'm asking you politely, Val, to mind your own business. OK? Now, here to spend time with me, or to placate Mama?"

"OK," Val said, shrugging her shoulders. "I get it, but please be careful. You have little Jessie to think about."

"Just a very old friend," Jenny replied, keeping her emotions under control. "I know what I'm doing, and he would never—"

"Never what?" Val pressed again. "Hurt you? I hope they don't turn out to be famous last words. Now, that scone recipe. Would you please show me how?"

-o-

"Why did you decide to take yourself off without me?" Lee asked over breakfast. "I thought we'd agreed to do stuff together, particularly in the holidays?"

"I told you," Jack said defensively, feeling very much as if he were under attack. "I wanted to see my grandparents because I don't usually get the chance, living here, and I'm concerned about their health and well-being. Anyway, you were busy with your … dad, as usual."

"Now that's not fair," she replied quickly, her anger

jumping to the surface. "If we spent all our spare time together, he'd be on his own. We're living in *his* house, for goodness' sake."

"And that's *another* issue," he replied, retaliating equally quickly. "Don't you think you spend an inordinate amount of time in his company, compared with mine?"

"Here we go again," she sighed. "Go on, then. What would you have me do?"

"Agree to buy our own house, for one thing," he said, shrugging his shoulders. "I don't feel good living in the same house, no matter how big it might be. We always, for example, have to wait until he's out before we can make love – behind closed doors – with half an ear cocked, in case. It's like having a child."

"Does it always have to come down to sex with you?" she shouted, now beside herself with suppressed anger.

"For goodness' sake," he muttered. "It was just an example."

Silence ambushed them quite unexpectedly, allowing them time to finish an unsatisfying and unenjoyable meal. By now tears were threatening her balance, as she picked aimlessly at the remnants of her breakfast, chasing bits of food around her dish with an ever more determined spoon.

Seeing her like this tore him apart. She was the woman he had married and promised to love for ever; the woman who would, hopefully, one day bear his children. He rose, plucked her from her chair, and drew her still protesting and rigid body to him. Normally, in a situation such as this, she would have melted into his arms, and they would have become as one. This time, it was different. She remained in his arms, but like a coiled spring ready to unwind once let go.

"Lee," he tried to soothe, "I'm sorry. It's just that things seem to have gotten a bit out of hand, what with—"

"So you bloody well should be," she exploded, pushing

him away. "I'm trying to make things right here – for us – and all you are doing is making it ten times more difficult. My dad needs me and—"

"I don't?" he asked quietly, saddened and taken aback by her unexpected and sustained outburst.

"But, you've got—" she protested, but stopped when she saw the sadness in his eyes – this man who had given her so much in such a short space of time. She began to realise what a hard time she had given him, and perhaps she needed to try to tell him what she was struggling with.

"Something I think you ought to know, Jack," she said, sliding her arm through his as she led him to their favourite settee.

"OK," he smiled as he sat down, relieved that *that* barrage had either subsided or had run out of ammunition. "I'm all ears."

"I think I'm pregnant," she said quietly, shuffling closer to him and looking into his eyes. She had realised some time before that Jack's eyes always betrayed his true feelings, and so it was here she always sought the truth.

"Did you just say—?" he asked, a look somewhere between shock and disbelief invading his face.

"Pregnant," she repeated emphatically.

"Think?" he puzzled. "Have you been to the doctor to get confirmation?"

"Don't need it," she said quietly. "I know."

"Then," Jack whooped, grabbing his wife and whisking her around the lounge in a show of ecstatic joy, "this calls for a celebration."

"Put me down, you big oaf," Lee said, grinning at his reaction. "You are pleased, then?"

"Pleased?" he panted. "Pleased? Of course I am. I'm delighted and amazed in equal doses. Do you know something, my wonderful wife?"

"Go on then. I'll fall for it," she laughed, joy trickling

back into her life. "What?"

"I'm ... going ... to ... be ... a ... dad," he shouted in glee, jigging around the room again, still holding his wife.

"Oh, my God," he continued, sitting on the settee with a bump as the realisation finally hit him. "How did this happen? I mean—"

"I think you know how, my dear," she answered, a coy smile growing in her face.

"Don't we need to tell your dad?" Jack said, an uncharacteristic outpouring of benevolence overcoming him. "When's he due back?"

"Well," Lee said quietly, a look of uncertainty beginning to cloud her face.

"I—"

"He knows already, doesn't he?" Jack said, his excitement evaporating as quickly as it had appeared. That sad, betrayed look that Lee couldn't help but recognise, settled on him like a lowering cloud, obliterating his happiness as surely as a high tide over ribbed sea sand. "I can't believe you told him before you told me."

His thoughts flicked back to that chance meeting with Jenny, and, amidst this inexcusable turmoil of uncertainty and illogicality, his mind began its long journey of rationalisation about his future direction. No one but Jack would know the outcome until that first physical step was taken.

Chapter 3

The last few days of the summer holiday saw Jack immersed in preparation for his new school. The job he had been interested in the year before had fallen through because of cuts and lack of money at local authority level. Yet, Jack's move away from primary to secondary had received a boost with his new post at Moor Secondary Modern. He couldn't believe that, in his mid-twenties, he had become the authority's youngest head of languages. Head of a department of one – himself.

Since Lee's dad had returned from his ancestry scouting trip to Kent, Jack and his wife had spent very little time together. The wedge that had begun to widen the gap between them hadn't been broached, or even mentioned in passing. They shared everything, as usual, in their lives – meal times, the occasional stroll in the park, bed – but, sadly for him, never as closely as before that fateful day her father appeared and took over her life. A pleasant and affable man on the surface, with a wealth of anecdotal experiences with which to entertain, Jack's depth of intuition, however, told him a different story.

Ron seemed unaware of the rift he had caused between the couple, but Jack sensed otherwise. His mind leaped back to his earlier comments about 'my baby is someone else's wife' and that she was all he had left in the world. Had he been subversively clever in orchestrating the rift?

Jack's intuition supported his initial doubts, and his feelings about people were very rarely wrong.

Unfortunately, he had no history from which he could judge, owing to their family distance. He wasn't too sure either about the real reasons for Lee's need to leave her beloved father and the place of her birth. Moving to the other side of the world had always seemed an extreme solution to a minor problem. Her fiancé had found someone else anyway, so was there something more sinister that had made her want to move?

Jack had always assumed Lee was an only child as she had never mentioned any siblings – until Ron let slip about John Pierre, one weekend over dinner. He noticed a stiffening change in her attitude and a frown cast at Ron, as she dismissed him quickly as a much older brother whom she hadn't seen since she was a little child. Although he said nothing, the doubts had begun to stack, and as he wasn't a scare-monger, he simply stored them away either to be dismissed or brought to light later.

"You never told me anything about John Pierre," Jack said casually as they shared a morning coffee and chocolate digestive break together, alone for once.

"Nothing to tell really," she replied quickly, a frown of irritation beginning to grow at the mere mention of her brother.

"Oh, come on, Lee," he went on with a friendly smile. "Nothing to tell me about the brother-in-law I didn't know I had? Well, for a start, how old—?"

"I don't want to talk about him," she snapped, the cup threatening to break as she slammed it into the saucer.

"Why not?" Jack persisted calmly. He wasn't about to take no for an answer this time. If there were skeletons, the cupboard's doors needed to be thrown wide. "Is there something you don't want me to know about your … precious family? Something … dodgy?"

Her reaction was frighteningly unexpected.

She shot to her feet, a murderous look of suppressed anger in her eyes, and deliberately overturned the coffee table scattering shattered crockery, broken biscuits and coffee dregs everywhere. Without saying a word, she stormed out of the lounge war zone and shut herself in her bedroom.

Throughout this debacle, Jack neither blinked nor moved, slipping into that state of mental invisibility he had inhabited many times since early childhood. Once the doors had rattled back to rest, he arose slowly, brushing crumbs and cup fragments from his lap and hair, and set about clearing the wreckage and putting the devastation to rights. He had seen this sort of stuff when he was a child. It didn't upset him then, and it hadn't upset him now. He was saddened, however, to think that his life might be about to follow history. If it did, he knew instinctively how he would react. This was not how he wanted or was prepared to live his life.

When the last vestige of shattered crockery had been consigned to the rubbish bin, the lounge door opened slowly and a remorseful and tear-drenched face crept around the frame. She rushed across the room, and threw herself at him, locking her arms about his neck as he drew her closer, soothing her as she sobbed.

"I am so sorry," she sighed. "I don't know what came over me, but it's just the mention of his name that incenses me so much. I *will* tell you about him, but not just now, if you don't mind."

"Don't worry about it," Jack reassured, stroking her hair as he drew her closer on the settee. "I simply thought you didn't want me to know about him because of something I'd said. So is it such a long time since you have seen him?"

"Jack …" she pleaded. "Please?"

"OK," he agreed. "Some other time, then."

His pragmatic mind took him mentally through the pressures and emotional warfare pregnancy might pour over her, but the vehemence and unexpected violence he had just witnessed worried him. Out of nowhere it had attacked, and with no warning – the natural stealthy assassin. This was an entirely new field of conflict for him. Entirely new and shocking, *this* aggressive confrontation was one he had not experienced in his relatively short life, and one for which he was entirely unprepared. Would that it was short-lived, particular to her physical state, and would not escalate from its present manifestation. He realised, however, that he could be skating on perilously thin ice.

His mind again drifted back to Jenny, as a wistful cloud softened the harsh edge of recent events. At first a guilty secret to be stopped at all costs, he now indulged his guiltless passion, allowing his mind to explore his feelings for her. After all, Jenny would never have treated him like this. *She* would have been proud to have been his, without demur or dissent.

"Jack?" Lee's voice cut through his musings.

"Mmm?" he replied, realising she had been talking and he hadn't been listening.

"You were miles away," she said, a puzzled smile on her face. "Your *other* woman?"

"Oh, aye," he replied, not showing any outward sign of how close she was. "My life-long affair with Diana Dors again. Just thinking about next week, what with the new school and all that."

"Worried?" she asked tentatively.

"Nar," he replied casually. "Be rayt. Need to get stuff into perspective and to stick to my plans for the year. It'll be fine. It's a job. Always got to remember that. It's part of my life, not all of it. Big mistake a lot of teachers make."

That was the last bit of wise advice his granddad had given him before he set off on his exciting adventure, apart from "Niver go aht wi' married wimmin". These were very wise words, and ones he would returned to throughout his teaching life.

"Cynical for you, Jack?" Lee said, a slight frown creasing her brow.

"Pragmatic and practical, I prefer to call it," he replied, a satisfied smile on his face. "Served mi granddad well, and he were a good man. Doesn't get better than that."

"I wish I'd gotten to know him better," she said half-heartedly.

"Still can," Jack replied sharply, batting the ball back into her court as he recognised her insincerity straight away. "They are both still reasonably hale and hearty, and they'd love to see you. Said so just the other day."

"Mmm," she replied, trying to deflect his deft response. "I think I'll get lunch ready."

She shuffled out of his grasp, and made for the kitchen slowly enough not to make it obvious.

"Thought not," Jack muttered, trying not to exacerbate an already delicate situation. "What am I going to do about you, eh Lee?" he added, almost under his breath.

-o-

The next day dawned, brutally red in tooth and claw, with Lee's body unconscious on the bathroom floor, a pool of red spreading slowly from her lower regions.

"Good God, Lee," he gasped, all vestiges of his night's sleep thrust from his head as he rushed to her aid. He realised immediately that something very serious was wrong, and that it had to involve their unborn child.

The ambulance arrived within minutes of his call, whisking her away with bells ringing and blue lights flashing. He followed in her Mini as quickly as the law would allow, arriving long after she had been rushed in to the hospital theatre to discover the worst.

"Come this way please Mr Ingles," a gently soothing voice took charge, guiding him towards a small waiting room at the end of a straight, dark green tunnel.

"My wife has—" he blurted out, once inside.

"Yes. I know," she interrupted. "She's in theatre now."

"But how—?" he gabbled, panic overcoming his usual calm pragmatism.

"We'll let you know when *we* know," she answered, turning sharply on her highly polished black court shoes, as she moved to the door, before he had the chance to question her more.

That was the start of the day from hell – one he would never forget. His worst fears were realised, and he had no idea why it had happened, or what he would say to his wife when she awoke.

-o-

"Things aren't rayt wi' yon lad an' 'is missus," Jud said to Marion as they sat at dinner the night Jack left.

"I think you're right," Marion replied as she served out her home-made steak and kidney pie.

"Ee lass," her husband grinned, "that looks almost edible."

"Cheeky bugger," she replied, pulling out her tongue playfully, knowing *his* sense of humour of old. "If tha doesn't want it, I'm sure t'birds will eat it."

"Nay, lass," he added very quickly, "I were onny jokin'. Here's mi plate, and don't be shy wi' yon spoon."

"I don't think she's iver been to see us, 'as she?" Jud mumbled through a mouthful of pie. "At least, if she 'as, I must 'ave been up t'garden or t'allotment."

"No," Marion replied, "she hasn't. Probably one of the reasons Jack's having a hard time of it. You know what he's like. Calls a spade a spade, and stands no messing. Easy going, and all that, until he's crossed. Slow to anger, and quick to calm down. But he doesn't forget – iver."

"Well, lass," he said appreciatively as he laid down his knife and fork, "that were rayt grand. Tha does a mean steak and kidney."

"But," she laughed, "tha's left nowt for yon birds."

"Birds eat seeds, lass," he replied in mock-seriousness. "They reckon nowt to pie."

"I suppose thy'd better 'ave this then," he added pulling a folded piece of paper out of his pocket. "Tha'll need to put thi glasses on, I think."

"What's this then?" she puzzled as she unfolded it. "A letter? From t'hospital? Addressed to thee?"

"Aye," he said, concern flicking over his face. "Came this mornin'"

"Then why didn't I see it this morning?" she asked, none too pleased he had kept it from her. "Not going to tell me?"

"Been ponderin' on it," he replied quietly. "Not too sure as to what it all means, does tha see, Marion?"

"Well," she answered slowly, "it says summat about yer lungs causing concern, and they want to 'ave another look. Appointment's day after tomorrow. Clayton Hospital in Wakefield. It's a good job we've nothing else on, or else there might have been a problem."

"Problem?" he laughed. "Summat else on? You mean other than bein' … retired, and havin' … nothin' else on?"

"What would happen if we'd been goin' away?" she said, standing her ground.

"Then we would 'ave 'ad to cancel…" he said quietly.

"Cancel mi 'oliday?" she burst in. "Never in a million—"

"Cancel t'hospital and arrange for another time," he continued unabashed. "Can't be that important, can it? They've already 'ad a look, told me what's up … an' I'm still 'ere, aren't I?"

"That's what concerns me, Jud," she said quietly, looking steadfastly into his eyes. "I want thee here. Tha's not been retired long, and I want it to be ... longer, tha sees."

"I do that," he answered quickly. "I had planned to be around to get under thi feet a lot longer, si thi, Marion, and this is a little blip that's not off to stop me just yet. All rayt?"

"Course it is," she answered slowly, "but si thi—"

"We'll find out soon enough," he said, very matter-of-fact. "Now, any chance of some o' yon rice puddin' tha's hidin' in that there oven? Or is that for thi fancy man?"

"How on earth tha can put away all that pie," she gasped, "and still 'ave room for puddin', I don't know."

"I'm a growin' lad," he guffawed.

"That's what I'm worryin' about," she came back at him, sharp as ever.

Chapter 4

Jack's new job at Moor Secondary School had been preying on his mind a little over the last week of his summer holiday. A small school for boys for whom a grammar school education hadn't been an option, it had been built in the early sixties to relieve overcrowding in its sister school at the other side of Leeds Outer Ring Road at West Park, and was designed for a maximum population of five hundred. Four storeys of glass and plywood housed most of the usual subject areas, with a separate smaller block for science, woodwork and metalwork.

Sparkling, shiny and new, it offered Jack an outlet for his organisational skills and creativity. However, although he was confident in his own abilities, a tiny seed of doubt spread small roots throughout his mind, as ever with a new path to his life.

"Mr Ingles?" an authoritative voice cut into his thoughts as he stood by the reception hatch waiting to be recognised as a new member of staff.

"Yes," Jack said, spinning round to confront the voice. "That's me. Mr Matthews?"

"John Rex, deputy head," the gruff voice replied in a pleasantly jovial way. "Would you like to come into my office where we might look at the day together?"

Jack remembered his first and only encounter with a deputy head at the start of his career a year or two ago. A couple of years? Is that all it was? Felt like he'd been at this game for an age.

John Rex was a much older man and bore an air of military authority. A thick mop of chestnut hair sat above a pair of dark tortoise shell spectacles, providing windows into dark brown intelligent-looking eyes. The real driving force behind the success of this organisation, there was nothing he didn't know about the school, the area, its parents and their off-spring.

"The students won't be in for another hour," he started, "so that gives us a goodly amount of time to sort out a thing or two."

"What about the others?" Jack asked, puzzled why he was the only one getting preferential treatment.

"You are the only new starter, Jack," the deputy explained. "I may call you Jack?"

"Course you can," he replied, an embarrassed grin attacking his face. "Sorry. I didn't realise I was the only one."

"Coffee?" Mr Rex suggested as a lovely young woman shouldered her way into the room, bearing a tray laden with a coffee pot, mugs, and a plate of cream cakes.

"Coffee and cakes?" Jack asked enthusiastically. "If this is the treatment I will receive every day, I'll stay during the holidays."

They both smiled as the young lady was replaced by a tall, grey-haired man who was a little older than the deputy.

"Mr Matthews?" Jack said, recognising the man who had interviewed him during the spring term past. "I didn't think the extra bun was for me."

They all laughed, and sat down to business, the most important part of which for Jack was ... coffee and cakes. He knew what was expected of him and what sort of youngsters were going to walk through his door – he had done his homework. All other protocols and programmes he would learn about soon enough. He couldn't possibly have been expected to assimilate more than a fraction of the stuff thrown at him by the double act, Rex and Matthews, so at least half of what he had heard he dropped into his mental 'pending tray'.

This particular day spurted and dragged in more or less equal measures, although break and lunchtimes were interesting.

"You'd be Jack Ingles, then," a small bespectacled man said while syphoning a cup of hot tea from the staff room urn at the beginning of the hour and a half lunch break. Most of the all-male staff had brought sandwiches which they dispatched with great speed to allow maximum time to indulge a shared passion.

"Yes I am," he replied, "and you are—?"

"Jim Stephenson," his companion answered as he dropped a fifth teaspoon of sugar into his steaming, giant-sized mug. "Do you play?"

"Play what?" Jack replied, puzzled at the question.

"Play what?" Jim guffawed. "Bridge. What else is there?"

"Well," Jack hesitated, drawing his long evenings in his college hostel's bridge school back from the depths of his memory, "as a matter of fact, I do."

"Excellent," Jim whooped sharing this momentous discovery with several other faces in the room. "Only, you replaced one of our players when he retired, and we were hoping you would replace him in every way when you were appointed. I *knew* you were the right man for the job."

He sat down at a square table, drew out a packet of untipped Park Drive, and, drawing on one deeply, he beckoned Jack to try the vacant easy chair for size. Mug of strong tea in hand, he obliged with a huge grin, cracking his knuckles as he sat in anticipation before picking up his already-dealt hand. This was going to be fun.

"Ken Childs will be your partner," Jim said, head swathed in a helmet of blue smoke, "and Bill Jones here will be mine. Here goes, then."

"Are we playing for money?" Jack asked, exciting a sharp whistled intake of breath from his companions.

"Not allowed," Bill said. "Education department rules. Why do you ask? Are you any good?"

"Well," Jack replied, touching the side of his nose with his forefinger, as a wicked grin crept into his face, "we had a bridge school at college, and I never lost any cash. Playing for money wasn't 'allowed' there, either. You catch my drift?"

"Yes!" Ken said, punching the air with both hands. "About time I had a bit of luck."

-o-

"An interesting day," Jack muttered under his breath as he strolled out of Parkstone Avenue on to the busy Outer Ring Road, a ten-minute walk to his bus stop.

"Hello, Mr Ingles," a small voice broke into his reverie.

Jack turned sharply, not expecting to see anyone once he had started his hike for the bus. A small boy of about eleven stood before him, smartly dressed in what could only have been a new school uniform – the uniform from Jack's new school.

"Hello," Jack replied, a smile on his face. "Although you are obviously from the Moor, I don't recognise you at all. My first day, you see."

"Mine too," the boy replied unabashed. "My name's Terrence. Terrence ... Ingles."

"Good Lord!" Jack burst out, a huge grin betraying his pleasure at their sharing a name. "Not my dad, are you?"

"Good gracious, no," Terrence replied, appreciating Jack's humour, "although you could be mine – if I didn't know *my* dad, that is, and I know that he's at home, waiting to give me my tea."

"Good for your dad, I say," Jack added, "and I have to say that I am very pleased to meet you Terrence Ingles.

Anyone who bears my name, and who could be part of my extended clan, has to be a good person. Us Ingles have to stick together. Don't you think?"

"We sure do," Terrence added, as if he had known Jack all his life.

"Your family from round here, Terrence?" Jack asked as they reached Lawnswood roundabout. "You know ... originally?"

"No," he replied. "We came here only a few years ago, from Castleford."

"No," Jack gasped. "Then that makes us almost family. I'm from Normanton. What's your dad's name?"

"Albert," Terrence replied.

"I have a Great Uncle Albert," Jack said, a smile of triumph on his face, "but I've not seen him for a lot of years, and he's probably too old to fit."

"Oops," he carried on, breaking into a trot. "Sorry, Terrence, but there's my bus. Got to go. Finish this conversation tomorrow?"

The last he saw of the lad was an excited wave and a huge grin as the bus rounded the corner in to West Park, on its way to Headingley and town.

"Well, even more interesting," he advised himself. "I wonder what tomorrow will coax out of the woodwork."

"Beg pardon?" a thin high-pitched rasp, like wind blowing over the edge of a taut blade of grass, invaded his senses. "What was that you said?"

A short, balding man, wearing a hair piece comb-over stood before him. His quizzical eyes and brows were very much at variance with the bus conductor uniform and ticket-printing paraphernalia around his neck and shoulders. Even more strange were the light brown sandals he wore over a pair of electric zig zag black and white socks.

"Sorry?" Jack said, puzzled at the question, until he realised that the little man wasn't supposed to have heard his thoughts at all. "Oh, yes. Sorry. Just thinking aloud I'm afraid. Single to the market, please."

Unconvinced, the conductor took his money and thrust his ticket unceremoniously into Jack's hand, a quizzical and disapproving raise of one eyebrow signalling his concern.

If he was lucky, and the bus driver was worth his salt, they would reach town in reasonable time to catch the half past four bus to Roundhay and home, but for now he had to be content with people-watching as the bus chugged through interminable traffic lights in Headingley, around Shaw Lane, the Arndale Centre and beyond. Apart from school, Jenny was the one image that consumed most of his quiet time, particularly when there was nothing else to fill the void. He wasn't sure about anything anymore. Although she had been his one true love of the last couple of years, he felt Lee slipping away from him. He didn't know how she felt about him either. It seemed that her one concern and care was for her father, although Jack felt sure she would have denied it had the subject arisen. Would they last much longer as a married couple, and—?

"Kirkgate Market," the squeak warned all on board. "Terminus."

His attention crawled out from within his inner thoughts as he craned his neck to verify his whereabouts. He wasn't sure where he was, engrossed as he had been with Jenny's company. She had begun to live in his mind, becoming real at each turn because he 'knew' how she would have reacted at everything he experienced. Jenny was the *only* person since his mother, who understood him completely, and who could have given him the support he craved when at a loss for a decision on which path to take. Fortunately for him, these occasions were rare, making it all the more important to have the right direction to follow.

Would that she was there with him now.

-o-

"Daddy?" William's seven-year-old daughter Mary asked in that lilting drawn-out way she had of letting him know she had a grave issue on her mind that needed an urgent answer.

"Yes, my poppet?" he said. "What do you want and how much is it going to cost me?"

"Do I have an uncle?" she replied, ignoring his attempt at humour. William's humour had never progressed beyond the pathetic, and Mary knew this. "Only … we've been doing relatives at school today, and, as you've never told me, I just … wondered."

It was a rare day off and he had agreed to collect her from her primary school, barely four minutes' walk from home. It was a pleasure for him to walk her back, because, usually when he got home from work, she was already tucked up and asleep.

"Why do you ask, my pet?" William asked, more than a little surprised she was asking on this day of all days.

"Well," she started slowly, gathering her reasoning, "I heard you and Mummy talking the other day. I *know she* has a sister, even though I haven't seen her, and I heard her mention somebody called Jack. I put two and three together, and came up with your brother, called Jack.

"How did you work that one out?" he asked, flabbergasted at her reasoning. He also remembered a similar conversation about putting 'two and three together' with his little brother when *he* was about the same age. He had lost *that* conversation comprehensively, so he wasn't about to make the same mistake with his daughter. She had very similar traits to Jack's at the same age – straight-talking, pragmatic, honest, and intuitive; a female version of his brother. Could he cope with that?

"It stands to sense," she answered quietly. "Why would you talk about someone in the same breath as Mummy's sister if he wasn't *your* brother?"

"Yes," he said, not wanting to put her off, "I do have a younger brother, and he *is* called Jack. Why do you ask?"

"Because I've never met him," she answered quite seriously, "and I think I should. Don't you?"

He smiled fondly, as many of his memories of his little brother flooded into his mind. It had to be his mother's funeral when they had last met, and that wasn't good enough for his children. He agreed in his head that she *should* see her uncle, and hopefully sooner rather than later.

"What do you suggest we do then, Mary?" William asked. "What advice would you give me to make things better?"

"Telephone or write," she said seriously, certain that she had the answer.

"But we don't have either his telephone number or his address," William answered quietly.

"Mmm," she muttered, unusually lost for words for a little while. "I'll need to give that some serious thought."

William smiled as she gripped his hand tightly, almost as a reassurance that she *would* sort it out – so much like his little brother. It could have *been* him, except for the long blonde curly hair and frilly frock.

-o-

Sitting in the lounge looking out over the back garden, cup of tea in one hand and half-eaten digestive in the other, Jack's mind drifted to his brother, sister-in-law and their three children he hadn't yet met. He had always thought a lot about William in his own way, but had seen him only once since that time at his mam's recuperation at Lytham St Anne's. He had held a lot of angst and animosity against his brother on *that* day – the worst of his life – and had spent little time with him because of that flying visit. Whether immersing himself in his family was his way of coping with Flo's death, he didn't know, but that was three years ago, for goodness' sake.

Jack stiffened as the front door clicked and opened on protesting hinges. His wife, or father-in-law? A light tread across the hallway told him it was the former.

"You home, Jack?" her soft voice drifted through the open door.

"In here, love," he shouted. "Just having— "

"A cup of tea and digestive?" she smiled as she bent to kiss the top of his head.

Rising from his chair, he kissed and hugged her before heading to the kitchen to make a fresh pot they could share. Same routine every day; same kiss; same hug; same conversation. Then she was away upstairs to change. Her belly seemed to be growing by the minute, to such an extent that she found it difficult to bend, even at two months.

Not long to D-Day. He wasn't sure how he was going to manage with a baby in his life. Would Lee want to stop working altogether? Wasn't sure he could cope with *that*. They would have to see. In his mam's day, new mothers joined that exclusive band of stay-at-homes to fulfil their maternal duties seriously. The working mother was a much more widespread but recent phenomenon, shifting the onus of child care to someone else. It had always been looked on as the most important job, but now careers and extra earning capacities had shouldered their way in.

"Joey Bump getting you down, love?" he said as his wife lowered herself gingerly into her chair.

"Mmm," she sighed, "a bit. I'm exhausted. Never seem to be anything else these days. I'm not sure whether I'm looking forward to finishing work and having the baby. It'll certainly be easier to get about, and a lot easier making love."

"I don't know," he grinned. "Sex-mad some people. Have you thought about tea?"

"I don't know," she grinned in return. "Always thinking

about their bellies, some people. The short answer is ... no. Too tired."

"Well," Jack suggested, "I had thought of two options. Either *I* could cook you a sumptuous meal, or we could have a take-away."

"Take-away it is, then," she replied. "I fancy fish and chips and peas and gravy, with a cheeky little cup of tea to be followed by ice cream and chocolate sauce."

"I like this pregnancy lark," Jack said.

"Why? Because you like the idea of a son and heir?" she asked.

"No," he said, dodging out of range quickly, "because I can share all the food you like now, but didn't before."

He reached the front door in double quick time, ducking under the mini cushion that whizzed over his crouching form.

"Fish and chips and peas and gravy twice, coming up," he continued, snecking the door behind him. "At least some decent food ... and then whatever I want."

Jack had always loved traditional Yorkshire fish and chips, and he had grown to love them even more since being married to Lee, although he didn't get to have them as much. Absence? Fonder? Perhaps, but some of her concoctions left a lot to ... be desired. She wasn't a bad cook, she just wasn't a ... good ... cook. Tinned potatoes, tinned peas, and tinned more or less everything else just didn't set his gastric juices racing.

How he dreamed about one of his mam's Sunday roasts, gravy drooling out of his mouth corners as he chomped his way through roasts and Yorkshire pudding. Heavenly. He could taste it all now.

Foreigners and people who didn't come from Yorkshire didn't understand the importance of good Yorkshire food to good Yorkshire folk. Unlike when he was a nipper, as a mature person Jack was prepared to give most foods a go.

He *had* to be adventurous to eat school dinners, it had to be said, but he drew the line at certain *in*edibles – offal of any sort, like the sick-invoking stuff glorified by his granddad, for example. Liver, kidney, brains, eyeballs, testicles and tripe turned his stomach at the thought. Even sniffing it was enough to make him throw up. There was no disguising the textures and tastes of his no-man's-land of non-edibles, even though Jud always called him a softy for not trying it at least. He *had* tried it many times – in his head. It was bad enough there, but it wasn't going to cross his lips, no matter how hungry he might feel. He would rather eat his own toe nails.

Gnawing at his vitals, too, was the way Lee had fallen pregnant pretty soon after her miscarriage. Of little comfort was his grandma's home spun philosophy that everything happens to some purpose in life, and that he needed to be content Lee had survived to try once more. Jack would cheerfully not have put her through it again so soon, but Lee had insisted – and who was he, a mere man, to argue? She had looked so poorly and fragile when she came out of hospital, and now she looked even worse.

Chapter 5

This secondary teaching lark was very different from what he had been used to at Broughton, and stretched his ingenuity and resource to the limit in his early days. Although he had taught at his first school for only a couple of years, it had been more relaxed and maybe a little ... easier. He had seen his youngsters almost every minute of every day. Whereas here, he was lucky to see some of them an hour a week, and they weren't 'his' youngsters at all. Chalk and Cheese. Lavender and garlic.

Although the school provided them with a good level of education, and offered opportunities for their future, they were always made very much aware that it wasn't a grammar school. According to urban educational myth, *that* sort of school provided them with the best chance for success and for a future in an appropriate job.

Nothing could have been further from the truth.

These teachers held the deep belief that academia wasn't necessarily the best way for the majority of their students to secure a future. Learning how to conjugate the present subjunctive of some obscure French verb, for example, wouldn't necessarily secure or sustain a job in the local foundry or in an insurance office or as a bus driver. These teachers believed it was *their* job to develop the skills necessary to hold down a job in a chosen artisan field that made up at least ninety per cent of the work force.

"Can't bloody well believe it," Bill Jones growled as he burst into the staff room at eight o'clock on Monday morning, after a particularly pleasant weekend away in early April.

"What's the matter, Bill?" Jim Stephenson asked, a sardonic smile crossing his face along with ribbons of blue smoke drifting up from the smouldering cigarette he cupped lovingly in his hand. "Old lady left you?"

"Some little turd only broke into my mobile classroom down the drive," he grumbled, a slight grin beginning to surface.

"Cause any damage? Take anything?" Jim asked, amused at the idea. "Though what anyone would want to take out of *your* classroom God only knows."

"One forced window," Bill went on, grinning even further. "Nothing damaged. Nothing taken, as far as I can see."

"Then what are you grinning about?" Jim puzzled, sucking hungrily on his Park Drive.

"Well," Bill replied, "the little bugger had only written on my black board *'Mr Jones is a twat'*. Get that. **Mr** Jones is a twat."

The room erupted into a huge collective guffaw at this marked show of respect-in-abuse for their colleague. The legendary Mr Bill Jones, the only well-respected twat on the staff.

-o-

Jack was concerned about the state of Lee's health during the later stages of her pregnancy. She suffered from such severe back ache for much of the time that she had to finish work much earlier than planned, spending a lot of her days in physical and mental discomfort. She had no idea, of course, what to expect because her mother wasn't here to advise and support, as only mothers can.

Love-making along with all other normal functions between husband and wife had ceased because of its sheer logistical impossibility – and the discomfort it brought to Lee in particular. This was not to mention the reaction it excited in the unborn child.

Despite their somewhat strained relationship, largely caused by her father's over-dependence on her, and her pandering to his every whim, Jack had looked after her throughout, trying his hardest not to react to her aggravation and sarcasm. He knew how badly their sometime state of warfare would affect the child inside her, who urged to be set free, and he couldn't allow anything to happen to him. It was strange that he was convinced it was a boy. He had no idea, but he was certain that he would soon be proved right.

Jack often wondered whether he could have foreseen or forestalled the deterioration of their once beautiful relationship, but blood ties ran too deep, and he felt, with hindsight, he never stood a chance.

The turning point was that fateful day when her father pulled in to her driveway. He had been taken aback by his sudden appearance and a little concerned at her reaction when she saw him – as if he hadn't existed at that one brief moment. Jack being Jack, he stored it away in the inner recesses of his mind, and forgot about it. Unfortunately for him though, he couldn't forget about anything. His 'stored' memories regularly returned to haunt him. Ron's was one of those annoying and uncontrollable things that stuck, and it wandered around his subconscious mind, surfacing periodically to confuse and irritate.

Still, he couldn't change any of that now. He could only try to recover some of what they had had at the beginning of their relationship. Yet, his last image of Jenny wouldn't be stilled. He knew in his heart that that's where his future *should* lie, and where it should have been from the start. What was he to do?

"Jack!" Lee's voice cut through his dreams as he sipped his tea and nibbled his digestive over his French marking.

"What is it, love?" he said, leaping to his feet, startled at the panicked look on her face as she stood over him.

"I think my waters just broke," she said, more than a little fear and apprehension edging her words.

"Hospital then," he said, leading her to the hallway, her coat, and her bag which was packed ready. He wasn't taking any chances this time. "You sure? Ready to travel?"

His calm, pragmatic and cool exterior was designed to convince her he was in control and knew where they were going. He was very good at hiding his emotions, fortunately, which gave her the confidence to accept the inevitable with equanimity.

The night air was cool and fresh, although her Mini was a bit cramped as he bundled her belongings into the back seat. Calm as ever in stressful situations, Jack helped his wife into the passenger seat.

'This isn't going to be easy,' he thought, dreading what the night was about to drop into his lap. He wasn't the one whose pain threshold was about to be stretched to its limit, but he did have qualms in his own way.

"Can't you go any faster?" she urged. "The pain's getting worse. Come on, Jack. Foot down."

"It's a thirty zone," he explained. "Not allowed to—"

"Emergency, for God's sake man!" she yelled. "Get a move on! You and your bloody rules will be the death of me. Bugger the laws, and get me to that hospital – now."

Jack had never seen her like this before, but then he'd never seen her at this stage of pregnancy before, either, about to drop their first infant. He hoped desperately she would hang on to it until they reached relative safety. He didn't feel like testing either his catching skills or his delivery techniques.

"This way, Mr and Mrs Ingles," a cheery voice greeted

them as they were spun around the revolving doors and spat into the hospital reception. "I think you'd find things easier if you sat in this wheelchair. Take the weight off both of you for a bit. Only space for one, I'm afraid, Mr Ingles."

The nurse smiled as she guided them towards the delivery area, where Jack was ushered into the waiting room, his job done. All he had to do was wait until told otherwise.

"You'll be all right in here, Mr Ingles," she assured him. "Mrs Ingles is on her way to the delivery suite to have tests before she goes into the labour ward. Not to worry. Soon be over."

Very firmly and without nonsense, the nurse ushered him into a similar ten feet by ten room, which was starkly furnished with six uncomfortable-looking chairs, and a small round table upon which were strewn women's magazines dating from the mid-1950s. In a waiting room which would largely be occupied by prospective fathers, Jack wondered why there would be a need for women's magazines. One three feet by three window gave out on to a small inner courtyard with three large pots of wilting plants waiting, praying for rain.

However he was about to cope with the next umpteen hours of incarceration in this airless, featureless and soulless dungeon, he didn't know. Except that he was Jack Ingles, and he always found a way.

'Well, Mam, me owd love,' he thought, bringing back the sort of conversation he might have held with Flo, 'a right pickle and no mistake, eh? How did this happen?'

'If you don't know *that*, my sweet boy,' she would have said with a smile, 'then I worry about you.'

Ee, the conversations he had missed would have broken his heart had it not been for Lee, and *she* was hell-bent on dropping a new responsibility into his lap almost imminently. Was he going to cope?

'Will I cope, Mam?' he asked her. 'How will I know what to do?'

'You'll know, my Jack,' she answered. 'You always do.'

"Mr Ingles?" a quietly soft voice tried to break into his own world. "Are you all right, Mr Ingles?"

"Sorry?" he answered, turning to see a young nurse by the door. "I was miles away."

"You perhaps might be better going home," she said. "It looks like it might be a long night. Baby's not ready to join us yet for a while."

"B–b–but, my wife—" he stammered.

"Will be fine," she reassured him with a smile. "She's in good hands. Promise. Go home and come back first thing in the morning. If we need you, we'll phone."

"Well, if you're sure," he said, unconfident in his reply.

The night air was welcome after the cloyingly sterile environment he'd just escaped. He stood by the car outside the maternity hospital near Leeds University, staring across the city skyline into the blackness beyond, the stars winking at him knowingly, telling him that all would be fine in the morning. He waited a few more moments, allowing the sharpness of nature to clear his tubes. Somewhere close by a dog barked its annoyance at being turfed out to its kennel, and the harsh response from an itinerant urban fox underlined for Jack the closeness and contradiction of nature, even here in the middle of town.

As soon as the Mini's engine burst into life, Jenny jumped into his head. Amidst all of this, the love of his life was with him, talking to him, holding his hand, soothing away the anxiety and stress. Although it was obvious where his feelings and thoughts *ought* to be on the eve of his child's birth, he couldn't get his childhood sweetheart out of his thoughts – that this should have been her, and he should have been sharing this first-born with *her*.

-o-

The first chore after a relatively sleepless night, was to let school know that he wouldn't be in for a couple of days; two in the first instance for the birth and then another two to take the new family home. *Then* the trials, tribulations and thrills of parenthood would kick in. He wasn't sure whether he would be ready for all *that* entailed – if ever.

"Whatever time you need, Jack," John Rex the deputy told him.

"Well," Jack replied, "that's very good of you, John, but I'm allowed two and two, and that's what I'll take. I'll be back the day after tomorrow, initially. I've left work for all my classes, just in case, in my cupboard in the classroom."

The school had never had anyone so well organised before, or so fastidious, to be honest. They appreciated everything had to be just so for Jack, and so accepted him as a package. According to one of the younger admin assistants, he was 'cute'.

However, it was unfortunate for the school that, although interesting in a very different way, this sort of teaching wasn't stimulating enough for him, and by now, almost at the end of his first year at Moor, he was beginning to regret the move. He checked the staffing bulletins weekly to see if his first choice at Merton Grange Middle School might be coming up at any time. Unfortunately, so far, there had been no indication of this.

He had tried to persuade himself regularly that this was the tier of education that offered him the greatest opportunities, but he was an unconvincing liar. He knew immediately the thought entered his head that he was trying to convince himself of its truth, but he knew himself of old.

The conversation usually went something like, "Well, Jack, old chap, surely you can see the rightness of the argument for moving on in secondary, can't you?"

"I'll grant you there *are* advantages, but the question

you have to ask yourself is 'Do the so-called advantages outweigh the disadvantages?'"

"And the disadvantages are?"

"It's boring in the extreme, and I prefer working in an environment where I have flexibility."

"What about the flexibility of approach in secondary?"

"There is no flexibility of approach. You are moving always in the same direction – towards examinations."

And primary schools have…?"

"Flexibility of direction, subject and approach. Nothing better. I rest my case."

He had persuaded himself over and over that he ought to think of moving, but the right job hadn't dropped in his lap yet. The newly conceived nine to thirteen middle school sector *would* offer such opportunities, but the queue for jobs would be round the corner and down the next street. So what chance would an inexperienced youngster such as him stand in this very open market place? Food for thought, though. His granddad had always encouraged him to aim high.

"Go for it, Our Jack," he would say. "Tha niver knows what'll 'appen unless tha guz for it. Thy owes it to thissen to try thi best. Tha can ask no mooer o' thissen."

Breakfast time. What was he going to have today? What did he have every day, and had had almost since birth?

"Porridge," he muttered. "Yes."

Should he have what he usually made – enough for Lee and himself? Or should he – ought he – to make just enough for one? He had no hesitation in plumping for the former.

'You could never have *too* much porridge,' he always thought. His mam would have laughed at his predictability, although tutting playfully at his overindulgence.

Only when he had finished his most important meal of the day could he consider preparing for the unknown.

Fortunately, his father-in-law was away for several weeks, visiting relatives in Canada, so Jack had no-one else to entertain with endlessly aimless polite conversation. Luckily too, there had been no telephone call demanding his urgent presence at the hospital, which to Jack's simple and pragmatic reasoning meant an even path was being trodden, and that all was right with the world. His slight difficulty now was tempering his natural instinct for immediacy so that he would arrive at the hospital at the appointed time, without having to dally in the dungeon for too long.

"Perfect timing, Mr Ingles," that same soft-spoken voice greeted him as he approached the reception desk.

"Hello, Nurse O'Keef," Jack replied with a smile of concern and reservation. "Perfect timing?"

"Mrs Ingles has had a busy but unproductive night," she replied, "but now things seem to be moving since she was induced an hour ago."

"Induced?" he asked, scratching his head, his usual puzzled frown beginning to betray his concern. "What does that mean, and what's it to do with my wife?"

Upon explanation, the worry of the unnatural flooded his mind. Why did this have to happen to them? Why couldn't it have been like most others? What if…?

"Nurse?" he asked, just before she left him in exile in his empty dungeon again.

"Yes, Mr Ingles," she replied, a sweet, indulgent smile showing her white teeth. "What do you want to know?"

"I know what an epidural is and what it's supposed to do," he puzzled, "but why, when they've been induced, and what's it going to do to the baby?"

"Your wife's struggling to push the infant out, Mr Ingles," the nurse explained, "and the baby has been in there longer than he ought to have been, because it's overdue."

"The alternative?" Jack asked, his worried look

emphasising his deep concern.

"A Caesarean section if all else fails," she said quietly, "but it won't come to that. Don't worry."

"And what do *I* do in the meantime?" Jack replied, shrugging his shoulders. "Just … wait?"

"I'm afraid so," she said, turning smartly towards the door. "Can I get you a cup of tea, or something?"

"Pint of Guinness?" he smiled.

She laughed as she closed the door on his dungeon once more.

Alone again. Naturally.

Chapter 6

"Well, Jack," Bill Jones grinned as he walked into the staff room, "you look like shit. Sleepless nights not doing it for you?"

"I never signed up for this," Jack groaned, yawning. "I wouldn't mind so much, but he sleeps during the day and wakes up at night. I think he must be a bloody owl, for God's sake."

"Does he respond to music?" Bill asked.

"Don't know," Jack said wearily, "but he does shut up when I switch the Hoover on. It's not that easy trying to sleep to a Hoover, I have to say. Haven't got a record player – just a radio, and they don't play music throughout the night, I don't think."

"Cassette player?" Bill suggested. "I just happen to have a spare, if that's any use?"

"Mmm," Jack said, raising his eyebrows. "Sounds like a plan, Bill Jones. You might just have leap-frogged to the top of my Christmas card list."

"What sort of music does he like?" Bill asked with a wicked smile.

"Soothing lullaby, I hope," Jack replied, a guffaw erupting from his mouth, "or country and western, or jazz, or opera. You'll get my vote for God the next time the position's up for grabs."

"Ready for Thursday?" Jim Stephenson chipped in as he

drew on his second Park Drive within the fifteen minutes he had been in the room.

"Thursday?" Jack asked, casting a twinkled, conspiratorial glance at Bill, who shrugged his shoulders in seeming ignorance. "What's happening Thursday?"

"You *have* remembered that on Friday," Jim replied, rising to his sarcastic best, "we achieve our just rewards in this meagre life?"

"No idea what you are on about, my old son," Bill interjected, deadpan.

"You've got to be joking me," Jim went on. "You are jesting – aren't you? Parents evening Thursday? Break up Friday? Six weeks' hols start Saturday?"

"Yes, Jim, old chap," Jack answered, a heavy cackle bursting from his lungs, "we are."

"You ba— " Jim bellowed, a huge cloud of blue smoke exploding from his face. "May the Lord smite you down with a Jew's ass bone."

"I think you'll probably find the saying is 'with an ass's jaw bone', old man," Jack laughed. "I hope you realise also that it means no bridge for six whole weeks."

"Ah, well now," Jim started with an uncharacteristically quick response, "*I've* joined a bridge club, I'll have you know."

"Does that mean you'll always be on the losing side then?" Bill answered as quickly.

"And," Jack chorused, "you'll not be able to cheat?"

"My wife has promised to join with me, too," Jim said, a look of smug satisfaction overtaking all. "Neither of you can boast a wife taking part and supporting you in *your* interests and pastimes."

"Wouldn't want her to," Bill replied, a wicked wink weaving its way into the conversation. "She's got her own interests, like ... looking after the home and seeing I'm well fed, and ... you know ... Besides, I have two daughters, so what time do *I* get for pastimes, anyway?"

"And my kid's barely out of the womb," Jack added, wiping the metaphorical sweat from his brow, "so what time do I get even for sleep, let alone hobbies? Can't wait to get back here."

"It appears, then," Jim added with finality and a huge grin of satisfaction on his smug face, "that I'm the luckiest man on God's earth."

"Either that or Esther wants to keep an eye on you, and a lid on your excesses," Bill added with a chuckle.

Jack almost choked on his morning tea, as they all laughed at Bill's subtle funny. Jack wasn't too sure how things were going to pan out this looming holiday. Six weeks with a new son he'd never had to cope with before, and a wife whose loyalty, allegiance and emotions he wasn't sure of anymore, didn't fill him with joy.

His mam would have loved this little lad – his little Sam. Lee had wanted to name him Ronald, after her dad, but Jack was having none of it. *He* had insisted on Sam, although it had caused tension and unease. Jack, however, had the ultimate say, because *he* had been the one to register his birth, and *he* had entered the name *he* wanted

Truth be known, George had been his first choice, after his granddad, but he knew she wouldn't go for that. It wasn't worth the aggravation and arguments it would generate. So Samuel – Sam – it was. There had been a few starchy days afterwards but she had gotten over it – so he thought. He was beginning to learn that he couldn't read his wife at all these days, and couldn't forecast her reaction at any time.

Still, 'life is what you make of it' was one of the 'home lies', as his mam used to call them, that she used trot out regularly, and he wasn't about to try to prove her wrong now. Two more days remained of this academic year before he could put that to the test, and he would know how things stood with Lee. Was he looking forward to it? He had mixed feelings. He was glad to be out of school for six weeks with his new son, but wasn't sure about his wife. Her father had returned from Canada, so it was likely she would want to be spending time with him. He had no idea what the state of his marriage would be by early September.

"Anyhow, Jack," Bill Jones asked at morning break as he sipped his coffee, "how's the new house coming along?"

"Bog-standard Wimpey detached box with a hugely long garden with little exciting to recommend it," Jack answered. "Gardening's not my thing, but it must be started this summer, because that's when we move in."

"Bit of advice, my boy?" Bill added. "Hasten slowly."

"With a wife as impatient as mine?" Jack said. "Not a snowball's chance in hell."

"Put your foot down," Bill went on. "She'll learn."

Wise words from an experienced married man no doubt, but would he have the brass neck to heed them?

"Good morning everybody," John Rex's deep voice rattled the door way. "Everyone well, I hope – enough to meet the challenges of our last two days until September."

Mutters from some quarters and cheers mixed with hoots of derision from others greeted the deputy's entrance.

"Registration awaits," he went on. "Go to it, gentlemen, go to it … and don't forget tonight."

"What's tonight?" Jack asked Bill in an audible whisper.

"Heard that one before, Jack," John interrupted with a smile, "many times. Not even remotely funny now. Class, please?"

"You're a hard man, John Rex," Jack threw over his shoulder as they breached the door.

"I've not got where I am today—" His last words were engulfed by the cacophony of boys' voices, eager to be back in school for their penultimate day this academic year.

–o–

"And Terrence's Uncle Albert is really his Great Uncle Albert," Mrs Ingles said, impressed by the young man before her.

"No obvious link then … yet," Jack replied, an air of disappointment covering his serious face, "but I'm sure there will be soon."

"Terrence really likes your lessons," she continued, "learning a foreign language, being with a teacher who has his name, and your sense of humour. Fantastic."

"He's a very good student, is your Terrence," Jack said. "Smart, well-behaved and personable. He'll go far once he has left school, with good qualifications. Occasionally, he needs to be careful whom he chooses as friends, but apart from that, it's a big thumbs up from me."

"Thank you," she went on. "It's because of you he has begun to like school again."

That last remark puzzled Jack, but he didn't pursue it. This sort of comment made his decision about his future career all the more confusing and difficult. There were aspects of what he was doing now that intrigued him and which he enjoyed, but was he getting the same satisfaction? Was he letting kind, flattering comments blind him to what he had always considered his calling? The proposed middle school development would be champion – if it ever got off the ground.

"I'm sure we'll find an ancestral link somewhere, and then," Jack grinned, "we'll be family."

One more day, then six blissfully lazy weeks of pretending to be rich enough not to have to work. He wasn't sure how Lee was going to react to his being there full time, what with a relatively new baby now dictating their lives.

Jack quite enjoyed the interaction with his parents, having put a good deal of thought and preparation into their interviews. Once finished, however, he had declined the usual offer of a couple of pints in the local in favour of catching the late bus home. He was one of only a handful of teachers who didn't arrive by car, and for whom that bus ride was a blissful release from the stress of being on top note all his working life. He could do without the madness and mayhem that modern-day driving added to it.

The air was clear if a little warm, but felt good against his still perspiring face. No matter how many windows you opened at this time of year, with so many bodies waiting anxiously to hear about Johnny's progress, it always felt cloying and sticky. Although it was still almost full daylight as he walked to his usual bus stop, it felt strange and almost eerie.

With buses every half hour at this time, he wouldn't be back home until gone ten – time for a cup of tea and a sit down for half an hour before bed. His son would have been asleep for a long time, so he wouldn't even be able to enjoy their usual playtime together.

'Never mind,' he thought. Six weeks holiday would give him plenty of time to see his Sam, and would be more than enough to compensate for the time he had missed that evening.

"And what time do you call this?" Lee's stern voice greeted his snecking the front door. "Been to the pub, no doubt?"

"Hello, love," he replied, his sarcasm not helping the situation. "Nice to see you, too. As it happens ... no, I didn't accept their invitation to a couple of pints in the Three Horseshoes. I didn't finish until nine, and, since then, I have been on the two buses I have to catch to get home. I don't have a car of my own, you see. Now let me think – where was our car? Oh, yes. You had it – just in case."

"*My* car," she corrected sharply. "I needed to use it ... with Sam."

"Ooh, we are getting possessive," he snapped back.

"Do you realise I have had to look after and amuse your

son all day?" she huffed, not best pleased with his attitude. "And what gives you the right to tell me what to do with my car?"

"Not getting any further into this," he said. "I'm off back to school in just over eight hours. So, I'm going to make missen a cup of tea and have a diges— "

"None left," she shouted.

"But there were— " he gasped, not believing what he was hearing. No digestives?

"My dad ate the last ones," she added quickly, seeing the incredulous look on his face, "and I've not had time to get any more."

"Not had time?" he growled, his anger rising. "And you've had all day ... with a car standing on the drive?"

"You don't seem to realise how much of my time the boy takes," she pleaded, trying to defend her actions. "Besides, I have housework to do, and ironing ... and— "

"You do it all again, do you?" he guffawed sarcastically. "Only ... the last time I looked ... it was me who did all that. Oh, by the way – and cleaning the windows, and— "

"Enough," she screeched, slamming her tightly clenched fist into the cushion next to her.

"What's going on?" another voice joined in from the hall doorway. It was Lee's father, just returning from his card school with his friends. "Lee?"

"Just being berated by your daughter for being late home from a parents' evening," Jack said, turning towards Ron, "by corporation bus."

"There's no need, surely," her father said, defending his daughter. "You have a car standing in the drive—"

"Which your daughter won't let me use," Jack retorted. "Do I try to fly to school? One of the few things I don't do in this place."

"No need to be sarcastic," Ron replied, moving towards his daughter. "She perhaps needed it to—"

"It's not moved all day," Jack interrupted. "Besides, this is none of your business, so keep your nose out."

"Now just a minute, young man," Ron shouted aggressively. "Don't you talk to me like that. This is my house."

"And there stands the problem," Jack replied, a deprecating grimace on his face. "Your daughter. Your house. Your terms."

"You know where the door is, and you—"

"Can leave at any time?" Jack interrupted again. "Wouldn't you both just like that? Lee?"

Jack turned towards his wife, throwing a questioning, reproving look at her, daring her to reject this unasked question. She shot quick glances at both her father and her husband, but looked down at her fingers without saying anything.

"So, I have my answer at last," Jack said quietly, more than a little angry at his father-in-law, and very sad that his wife had finally rejected him as a husband, lover, and father of her son. She had made her choice, which she would live to regret.

He slept fitfully on the settee that night, bitterly regretting he had ever agreed to live with her father, remembering the qualms he had tried to share with her. She hadn't been interested in finding a house of their own because she was still as emotionally and inextricably tied to him as perhaps she would ever be. Their prospective new house away from her father seemed to have tipped her over an edge. How was Jack going to cope with that situation?

Jenny would persist, however, in muscling her way into his subconscious and conscious minds. She drifted into his dreams, and when he awoke, she was there, reminding him of his promise that they would be together … one day. How he wished that 'one day' was this day.

-o-

Games and activities with no purpose other than to occupy and pass the time as quickly as possible, allowed Jack's day to whizz by quicker than he had hoped. He neither relished nor cherished the thought of returning home to some sort of atmosphere from which his holiday might never recover. Having slid out of the front door noiselessly before Lee had awoken, had ensured that he hadn't seen his wife since late the night before.

Unbeknown to him, she had heard his shuffling about, hoping he would come to her to at least start the recovery process. When he didn't, she began to weep in silent sorrow at what she had done to him the night before. She couldn't explain why she had allowed her father to railroad her into silent support of his reaction to her husband. Now she would have to wait a whole day to try to make things right.

She had no idea that their relationship was well on its way to a point of no return.

He slipped his briefcase behind the hall's hat stand as he sidled through the front door as quietly as he could. He knew his wife would sense his presence no matter how quiet he thought he might have been, particularly as he had dropped one of his shoes as soon as he had taken it off. He slipped his jacket on to the hat stand, and, as he turned towards the lounge, two urgent arms drew him towards a soft, warm body and a pair of soft, wet lips.

"I'm sorry," she said after their urgent love-making, which had taken him by surprise.

"What for?" he said, trying to be funny. "For doing that?"

"No, silly," she smiled, "for allowing my father to treat you like a common interloper. I shouldn't have done it, and I've no idea why I did. Can you forgive me?"

"Don't worry about it," he assured her, with more than a little disbelief in what he was saying. He knew it would happen again, once Ron was in control in his house.

The sooner he could get her out of his clutches and into somewhere that was theirs, the more of a chance he had of keeping his family together. His son was only a few weeks old, but Jack couldn't imagine life without him.

"These things happen," he went on. "No big deal, but I do think we need to have that place of our own. Don't you?"

"Perhaps so," she said, after a moment's hesitated indecision. "But what about Dad?"

"What about him?" Jack replied sharply. "He's a grown man, you know. Doesn't need looking after anymore."

"No need for sarcasm," she said, rounding on him angrily. "He is my father, and he does need my support. He looked after me when I was little, don't forget."

"…As do most parents," Jack shot back straight away. "It's sort of part of their job as parents, don't you think? Shouldn't your first allegiance be to our son and … to me?"

"You see," she said, eyes flashing, "there you go again. You can't even be civil when I've let you have sex with me. Aren't you ever grateful?"

"Oh, a reward, now is it?" he flew back at her. "Most couples do it because they want each other. You seem to 'allow' it as a means to getting your own way, by the looks of it. Why don't you stop all physical contact and be done with it? You never seem to enjoy it, anyway."

"Enjoy? Enjoy?" she screeched, her anger overwhelming her. "What's to enjoy? You don't satisfy me, anyway. Now, James—"

"James what?" Jack said quietly. "He did? But you always told me you didn't believe in sex before marriage. Another lie?"

"I didn't say I did," she replied defensively. "And besides, my relationship with him is – was – none of your business."

"It is if you did it with him before you reeled me in," Jack hit back. "It was one of the things that drew me to you. A woman of principle. True to her word. Means not a jot now, I'm afraid. If I'd only known—"

"You'd have what?" she snarled. "Not asked me to marry you?"

"I wouldn't have waited for you to come back from Canada," he said quietly. "Two virgins together, cementing their truly innocent relationship. Only … it was one-sided, wasn't it?"

"Wow," she quietened at last. "Six weeks of this. Are we going to continue to be like this? Bickering and flying off the handle at the slightest thing?"

"But, it's not the slightest thing, is it?" he replied quickly. "It's happening more frequently, and I can neither predict nor avoid it. We must do something, or life won't be worth living for both of us. I love you, Lee, and I'd like to get back to how it was."

"Me too," she said rolling on top of him again, and kissing him like it was the first time. He responded, making her gasp at his urgent penetration and the smoothness of his love-making. Despite all else, she wanted him, and he gave it to her like they'd not done it before. The following hour exhausted them both, but it was love-making like neither had experienced. They had been married for over a year, but they had only just experienced their first full-on sex that had satisfied them both deeply.

Sleep crept over them, taking them down drowsy lanes, until it sprang its not unexpected ambush, keeping them prisoner for an hour or two. All this time little Sam gurgled happily in his crib, oblivious to the relationship in turmoil that was unfolding around him.

Chapter 7

Sam was an absolute delight to be with as he began to fatten and grow, and this was the ideal time to cement their relationship. It gave Jack endless pleasure helping him to strengthen his legs, and to crawl, totter and walk upright. He was a quick learner, was Sam, picking up new things every day.

As his relationship with his son strengthened and grew, his relationship with his wife weakened and began to wither. Jack had known that the strong sexual attraction Lee and he felt for each other wouldn't be enough to sustain them. True to prediction, they began to quarrel more and love less, particularly when her father was home. Jack would often catch a self-satisfied smile on Ron's face following any confrontation with Lee, who seemed to become much more tense around Jack when he was there. On their own with little Sam everything was smiles, touching and feeling, and relaxed.

Jack had never been a quitter, but he knew in his heart that he was fighting a losing battle against Ron's influence over her.

"Not been to attend to mi Mam's grave for a few months," he said cheerily as he was giving Sam his breakfast. "So I thought we might bob across to Normanton tomorrow and give it a bit of a tidy. We could drop in to see mi grandma and granddad, and spend some time together in Haw Hill

Park. What do you say? We could take a picnic and—"

"If you don't mind," she replied nervously, "as Dad's going to Canada for a month within the next day or two, I thought Sam and I would stay here with him. You go and do what you have to do, and perhaps look up one or two of your old friends. Maybe stay the night at your gran's?"

"That's a disappointment," he said, not afraid to show his displeasure. "But, if I can't persuade you…"

"It'll be fine," she replied, visibly relaxing. "Besides, little Sam needs his routine, and at this stage things would be a bit awkward – if that's OK with you."

"It'll have to be, I suppose," he said quietly, not sure where this would take him. There was something niggling away at the back of his mind, as usually happened with Jack. Intuition? Vision? Sixth sense? Whatever it was, it always caused him disquiet. He felt that something unpleasant was about to happen over which he had no control, and which, he was sure, would cause him distress. It was that same feeling he had had when his mam died.

"I'll take the train," he went on, "because you and our Sam might need the car. Nothing worse than having to traipse when it becomes a nuisance, and our Sam can do without that."

"You are so kind and dear, Jack," Lee said quietly, putting her arms around his neck, "and so understanding. You deserve—"

"You and our Sam," he reassured her, drawing his wife close to his chest and kissing her tenderly, and, noticing a tear in her eye corner, he added, "No need to be upset, my lovely. I'll be back in a couple of days or so, and then we can plan a couple of days away at the seaside."

"Sounds good to us," she replied, almost under her breath.

"I'll catch the nine o'clock train, so I'll be off in good time," he said happily. "That'll give you two or three days to have time with your dad before he leaves. OK?"

"OK," she replied almost apologetically.

"Something wrong, love?" he asked her. "You seem a bit … quiet and reticent."

"No. I'm all right," she replied, forcing a smile. "It's just that it's a shame you won't see your son at the beginning of your long holiday, and—"

"It's only a day or two," he assured her with a smile. "I'll see you both soon. You're not going to do as runner are you?"

-o-

His train journey to his home town was the same as he had endured a thousand times before – alteration and improvement work being done in Leeds City station, the slow knickerty knack over the irritatingly slow points, the squealing grate of the Holborn Curve, and the smells of the various industrial plants en route. He could travel the whole journey with his eyes shut and know where he was according to his other senses.

"Bloody 'ell," Jud growled as he opened the door on his grandson. "Marion, quick! Call t'police. There's somebody big out 'ere, impersonating Our Jack."

"Ey up, owd cock," Jack laughed. "It's good to si thi. 'Ow's tha doin'?"

"Ah'm all rayt, tha noz," his granddad replied. "Same as allus. Niver any different. Fit as a lop."

"Is tha goin' to ask me in, then?" Jack asked, raising his eyebrows. "Sumbody in thiyer tha dunt want me to see, or summat?"

"Cooers not, daft bugger," Jud laughed. "Thi grandma's just purrin t'kettle on. Dunt suit 'er at all."

They both burst into fits of laughter, bringing Marion to the door.

"What's goin' on 'ere, then?" she said planting her feet

firmly on the floor and hanging her fists on her hips. "Not letting t'poor bairn in, Jud Holmes?"

"Jack," she sighed, hugging her beloved grandson. "It's grand to see you, lad."

"You too, Grandma," he said, kissing the top of her head. "I've missed all this – kissing my favourite lady. I'm sorry it's been a while, what with school and a new baby. I was going to bring him, but Lee wanted to spend some time with her dad before he goes back to Canada for a few months. I'll bring him to see you next time."

Marion cast a knowing glance at her husband who shrugged back at her as he dropped his gorilla's arm around his grandson's shoulders, and led him into their kitchenette.

"Now," he said firmly, "it's time for a cup of tea and—"

"A chocolate digestive by any chance?" Jack said hopefully, his eyebrows jumping up his forehead in anticipation.

"Now, what gives you that idea?" Marion smiled. "Anybody would think we were expecting you."

"Why would tha want biscuits when tha can 'ave … 'om-med scones?" Jud growled in satisfaction.

"Don't tell me tha's tecken up bakin' instead of allotmenting, Granddad," Jack guffawed. "Niver thowt ah'd see t'day"

"Course not, daft bugger," he replied, glee jumping into his face at the rerun of their shared repartee. "Thi grandma rustled 'em up earlier on, like. She were convinced tha were off to come today. Bloody psychic, if thy asks me. Ar could she know? Tell me that."

"Because she's mi Grandma. That's 'ow," Jack said deliberately. "No use asking 'ow. She just does."

"Any 'ow," Jud said after a moment or two's silence, "'ow come tha's 'ere today. Owt special on?"

"What do you mean? Apart from wanting to see you two at t'beginning of mi summer 'olidays?" Jack said, more

67

than a little surprised at the question. "I've come to see to mi Mam's grave, and to pay mi respects into t'bargain."

"And?" Marion asked, obviously wanting to explore her idea of his real agenda.

"And what, Grandma?" he said, seeming to be a little puzzled at what she was trying to suggest. "Do I need to have another reason?"

"Things aren't what they might be between you and yon lass at home, are they, lad?" Marion said, bluntly. Never minced words, didn't his grandma. Straight out. No corners. Always knew where you were with Marion. Brutally honest sometimes. True Yorkshire woman.

"Just one or two small issues like you get in most marriages, I think, like I told you last time," Jack replied after a slight pause, which convinced Marion she was right. Best left at that. She would find out soon enough. "Anyway, if it's all right with you, I'll stay a couple of nights, sort mi Mam's grave out in t'morning, and be off back to Leeds mid-afternoon on Friday."

"Course it is, lad," she assured him. "Thi bed's allus med up, so tha can come anytime thy has a mind."

"Can I treat you to fish and chips for tea?" Jack asked in anticipation.

"No, lad," his grandma said, "I've a nice bit of stew bubblin' away in yon oven. Wouldn't you prefer some of that ower fish and taty?"

"What do you think, Grandma?" he whooped in delight. "All this and heaven too."

-o-

The churchyard was deserted and a little chilly for early on a summer's morning. Standing close to the spot where he had held and kissed Jenny passionately, forced an excited shiver of expectation from deep inside. Half expecting to turn and see her standing, waiting for his arms to draw her close again, he shook his head in disappointment when it didn't happen. Her last words, however, drifted back into his thoughts…

'18 Queen Street' drew his mind even closer to her. He wanted to hurry there, to knock on her door, have it opened gingerly, and for her to be standing before him, a smile of satisfaction on her face. He couldn't. He shouldn't. But he knew he would once he had finished with the grave.

Queen Street was relatively busy for this time of day, he thought, forgetting that, although *he* had finished work for his summer holidays, not everyone else had. What if her daughter, Jessie, was there? She was only very young, so it didn't matter. Although, if she was half as sharp as her mother, she would know. Wouldn't she?

He was there, and so had to stop finding excuses not to call. Perhaps he should walk past the door, and return to his grandma's. Yes. That was it. Walk slowly past that inviting but dangerous door. Two steps past and his heart pounded in his chest. Nearly…

"Jack?" a very familiar voice spun him round. "It is you."

"Jenny," he gasped. "I was just—"

"About to walk by?" she asked urgently, not about to let him walk away again. Not now he was almost within touching distance. He had come to her. He had kept his promise, like she knew he would. She wanted him even more than she had dreamed, and now he was standing in front of her.

"Are you coming in, then?" she urged. "Or have you got another appointment somewhere else that doesn't exist?"

"No," he replied firmly, courage swelling in his chest. "No, Jenny, it was you I came to see, and I will come in, if that's all right with you?"

"I knew you'd come," she sighed, flinging her arms around his neck, once the door had been snecked and locked, and setting her soft, full red lips on his.

They kissed, gently at first, but passions swelled urgently as they undressed each other, not stopping kissing for a second. She drew him into her, and in that first moment of union, they were carried to a place neither had experienced, where no-one – nothing else – either existed or mattered.

Their love-making was long, gentle, exciting, and satisfying, where their bodies understood each other's needs, carrying them on a wave of ecstasy to a final overwhelming climax. Gasping, satisfied, and happy, they were loath to let go, both wanting to revisit and explore again and again what they had just experienced for that first time.

"Why haven't we done this before?" she gasped, every excited nerve in her body on edge, preparing to prolong the ecstasy as she rolled on top of him. "We were meant to be together from the start, and—"

She gasped as he penetrated her again, taking her to an even higher level of excitement she had never dreamed of reaching. She could do nothing but let it carry her along until it reached its natural, otherworldly climax, completely eclipsing the previous one.

"Jack," she croaked, tears streaming down her face. "Oh Jack, how could you do this to me? I can't lose you now, not after that. I…"

"I love you Jenny," he said quietly. "I always have, and I always will. I promise we'll be together soon."

She rolled over onto him again, slid her arm and head onto his chest, and sobbed.

"Are you … all right?" he asked, a note of confusion entering his voice. "Jenny?"

"I'm so happy," she sobbed. "These are tears … of happiness, to think we will be together at last. Stay here tonight? Please?"

"I'm stopping with mi grandma and granddad for the next couple of days," he answered, "but I'm sure they'll … understand. Tonight, and then I'll have to pop back to them tomorrow."

"Won't I see you again, then?" she asked, a note of panic invading her voice. "Will you be—?"

"Coming back here for tomorrow night," he assured her, rolling on top of her again. "And this is so you won't forget."

They giggled as he slid gently inside her once more, making her gasp with anticipation of what she knew was coming next.

-o-

The train back to Leeds was tediously slow. Line works and signalling faults delayed his return significantly. However, he couldn't get the last days with Jenny out of his mind. He had never felt like this with or about anybody else, and he knew now where his life must lie. He should have felt guilty, but he didn't. He felt it was meant to be, and should have happened much earlier. Yet how could he give up his son? Because that is what living with Jenny would mean.

Early evening saw him striding up the driveway past Lee's Mini, to an ominously dark house. She wouldn't be in bed at seven o'clock, would she? Neither would she be out past Sam's bedtime. So what … ? Where? Why?

"Hello, Lee," he called quietly, unsnecking the front door. "I'm back. Lee?"

Silence.

The house smelled like it hadn't been lived in for a day or two, and this raised his suspicions and his fears. Flicking the light on, he quickened his pace through the lounge, catching sight of an envelope on his chair. Stopping to pick it up, he recognised her writing straight away. The letter before him jolted him out of his Jenny cocoon to the reality that his wife had taken his son to Canada 'for a few months' to think through their situation.

A few months? She couldn't take his son away from him like this. He had a right to… To what? They were at the other side of the world, for God's sake, and he couldn't afford to chase after her. Obviously, it had been well planned and engineered by her father, who had managed to spirit them away while Jack had been at his grandma's. How stupid could he have been? It was now glaringly obvious they had orchestrated it all to give them time to leave, and he hadn't seen it coming. How naïve could he be?

He slumped into his chair, head in hands, and he knew in that one brief moment they wouldn't return, and that he had lost his son and his wife. They knew he couldn't – wouldn't – do anything about it. They knew he wouldn't even telephone. That wasn't Jack's style. He knew he couldn't afford it.

He lifted his head and sat back in his chair, a slight smile growing across his face. They had just made his decision about his future so much easier, and now it was clear, in his usual straight forward pragmatic thinking, what he was going to do.

"Jenny?" he said as the telephone connection came to life. "How would you fancy me coming to live with you?

"When? Well ... now.

"For how long? How about ... permanently?

"Jenny, calm down, don't get excited. I'll be there in about a couple of hours. Just got to throw a few things into a bag, jump into the car, and then I'll explain when I see you. We've a few things to sort out, a few calls to make tomorrow, and then a bit of house-hunting to do ...

"Jenny ... please don't cry.

"No. This is neither a wind up nor a joke. It's for real, my darling. You'd better believe it.

"Two hours max. You get the kettle on, and I'll bring tea."

Chapter 8

"You're not having me on, Jack Ingles?" Jenny asked, her naïve little face asking through a mouthful of Chinese egg fried rice and sweet and sour. "This isn't just a way of getting back at your bitch of a wife, is it?"

"Jenny." he replied a look of mock hurt flirting with his eyebrows. "How could you? Think about what we were doing before I found out. Do you remember? Was I having you on with all that? From what I recall, we both enjoyed all we had to give, and I believe you wanted more. Wore me out, you did."

"Right," she guffawed, a mocking tone in her voice. "You were never worn out in all this world. If I remember right, it was me who was worn out."

They giggled, pushing aside the remains of the take away, and grasped each other in a desiring clutch as they locked lips to express their love for one another at last.

"I can't believe we're here, where we should have been an age ago," she said, her head contentedly on his chest, sprawled out on the settee. "Didn't see myself living here, though."

"That's one of the things we can change," Jack said, kissing the top of her head, closing his eyes as the fresh, sweet smell of her hair filled his nostrils. "If you had the choice, where would you live?"

"I've always had this notion of living in a white cottage

in the country," she said, a wistful look clouding her eyes. "You know ... somewhere where we could raise our children in peace and contentment."

"Would you like more children?" he asked, gently stroking her hair, not knowing what her response might be.

"Your children?" she sighed contentedly. "Of course I would. Of course I do."

She kissed him passionately to reinforce what she had said, what she felt.

"I should like to have your children very much," she reassured him, gazing into his eyes.

"You do realise I should like to adopt Jessie as my own?" he said, out of the blue.

"Would you really do that?" Jenny said, her eyebrows betraying her surprise. "For me?"

"No, Jenny, not for you," he said. "For Jessie and ... for me."

"Jack Ingles," she sighed, tears welling again. "You always know what to say, and I love you for it. You don't have to. She—"

"Will then be my daughter too," he continued. "Our daughter."

She sighed comfortably as he continued to stroke her head and to caress the fine, downy hairs on the nape of her neck. It took her back to that first time, that first touch across a café table, which had stunned her, aroused her and made her want him even then. These feelings from his touch that shocked her into desiring him then, leaped into her body now. She didn't know then how she would handle such power, and now she didn't care to try. She wanted to allow those shocks of desire to take over her body and her mind forever. He was here because he wanted to be, and she wanted him to stay, making her feel alive and needed in a way she had never felt before.

"I want you, Jack," she murmured. "I want you to love

me like I was – am – the only woman you have ever loved. I want you now."

"You are the only woman I have ever wanted," he whispered as they caressed each other again. "The only one I have ever loved, truly."

Their love-making was easy, gentle, powerful and it caught them both up in a whirlwind of intense feeling and emotion, allowing them to luxuriate in exploring each other like never before. She didn't care what had been, or what was about to come, because she knew Jack – her Jack – would make it all right. She knew…

All other thoughts were driven from her mind as they reached their climax together. That was her Jack. Ever aware of her needs first and foremost … love-making she wanted never to end but not being able physically to sustain … until the next time…

"When's Jessie back with us?" he asked as they cleared away the debris from their tea.

"Day after tomorrow," she replied. "Why?"

"Well," he continued, "we've planning to do, decisions to explore, and … house-hunting to undertake. We can't stay here too much longer. Where would we put three extra kids, for a start?"

"Three extra—?" she said, her eyebrows shifting to the top of her forehead in shock and surprise.

"Only kidding," he chuckled.

"I was surprised because I had thought four," she threw back at him.

They burst out laughing together, happy in themselves, and in the new life that had just opened up for them. All Jenny's fears for the future had been wiped away when this man walked purposefully back into her life, and all her closed horizons exploded into infinity.

"Do you think your wife will ever come back with your son?" she asked tentatively, not really knowing what was in

Jack's mind. She knew him to be a straightforward man – simple, almost – who was honest to a fault, and she knew he would make the proper decision when the time was right. She didn't know, however, the relationship he had enjoyed with her, any more than he knew about Jessie's father. Would *he* ever return to the scene? It wouldn't matter if he did, because Jack was going to be Jessie's dad soon, and her natural sire could do nothing about it.

"I have a very deep feeling inside that she won't," he started, shaking his head solemnly, "but it makes no odds to me. She's made her choice, and, while I would never close the door on any relationship with Sam in the future, she's made his decision for him. You and Jessie are my main concerns now."

She hadn't expected that answer at all. Perhaps she didn't know him as well as she thought. She slid her arms around him and pulled him close to her.

"We'll look after you and love you from now on," she said quietly, trying to soothe away any hurt he might feel. "Jessie and me, we'll be your family … and David and Julie and Ellie and—"

"Bringing in the whole street?" he laughed, throwing his hands in the air. "I surrender."

"I want to have your children, Jack," she insisted, "and they will be the happiest children alive, because they will have you as their father, and we will love them and they will all love you back, Jack Ingles."

"I adore you, Jenny Ingles," he whispered. "Always have. Always will."

"What did you call me?" she asked, a surprised look invading her beautiful and now carefree face. "Jenny Ingles?"

"Isn't that what you'd like to be?" he said, drawing away, a little puzzled at her response. "I'm going to see the solicitor tomorrow in the High Street. I'm filing for divorce because my wife has deserted me in favour of living with her father in another country. End of chapter. Once that's been done, we can get married, like we should have done back then. I ought to have taken my chance that day you told me you were pregnant, and I rode away from you without so much as a backward glance."

"Wasn't your fault, Jack," she told him again. "I couldn't have expected you to take on another man's child."

"I'm doing now what I should have done then," he insisted, "only, getting on for five years too late. I'm lucky to have a second bite at the cherry. I'm not going to miss my chance of eternal happiness a second time."

"Just think," she said, squeezing his arm, a squeak of joy escaping her lips, "Jack, Jenny and Jessie Ingles ... we belong at long last."

"And you'll belong even more when we find the right place to put you in," he laughed. "Any objection to living in any of the posh Leeds suburbs?"

"Leeds," she gasped. "Objections? Away from this dump? No fear. Normanton's a lovely but going-nowhere town. Leeds would be ideal. Somewhere grand and big and palatial."

She twirled around on her toes, hands clasped above her head ballerina-like. The last time Jack had seen her so happy was the time they had spent together before she left for university, ready to change the world. Now, her world had opened out significantly, giving her the opportunity to live and grow, and to change forever.

"Hang on a bit," he laughed again. "Somewhere aspirational so we can move when our family grows, I thought? Probably three or four?"

"Three or four what? Windows?" she puzzled.

"Bedrooms, my sweet," he smiled. "One grand one for us, one for Jessie, one for David or Julie or Ellie, and a guest room for when your mum – or sister – could come to stay."

"Oo er. 'Ark at 'im," she said, mincing about all

lah-di-dah. "Guest room, eh? We *will* be grand."

"Nothing's too good for you, my love," Jack said quietly, thumbs tucked under imaginary trouser bracers as he flexed his knees in front of an imaginary open, roaring coal fire.

"Do you realise," she said, a note of surprise in her face, "that it's gone one in the morning?"

"Doesn't matter," he said. "We're on holiday, and that means we are allowed to have a lie-in. Fancy a lie-in tomorrow?"

"I fancy a lie-in now," she insisted, grabbing his hand and leading him to the stairs as she flicked off the lounge light. "Tidying tomorrow … at some stage … if we have a mind. Or maybe we might…"

Chapter 9

"...And then we can get my decree absolute six weeks later," Jack explained. "There are rules and regulations, of course, but the legal bod seems to think it won't be too much of a problem."

"Rules?" Jenny asked, a little frown of disappointment dancing around her brow. "What regulations?"

"Well," he continued, "to get a divorce on desertion grounds, you have to have lived apart for two years or so, but he reckons we might go for unreasonable behaviour, which can allow an earlier release. He even suggested it might be worthwhile admitting to adultery to expedite the process. Not without risk because she may well claim costs, but as there is a no-blame clause, it should just squeeze through. Would it worry you if we had to wait a bit?"

"Course it wouldn't," she said, dismissing the idea. "You're mine now, anyway, so time has no meaning. Still, the sooner the better, I say."

"Then we'll let the law take its course," Jack said with finality. "Your mum needs to know as a matter of some urgency, and she'll tell your Val, no doubt, in her own good time."

"Which will be within two minutes of my leaving, if I know Mother," Jenny said, backing into the conversation. "And I do—"

"I shall have to tell mi grandma and granddad," he

said, "but I don't think it'll come as a surprise to them. I think Grandma sensed all was not well between Lee and me by the way she evaded coming to see them. For our get-together, I want you by my side. Would that be all right with you? They're my only living close family after William, and I need them to like you, which they will. How could they not?"

"Of course it would. Why wouldn't it?" Jenny replied firmly. "And if they don't like me—?"

"They will," he interrupted her. "They'll love you, and they'll be able to see how much we mean to each other."

"And Jessie?" she asked tentatively.

"Part of the package deal," Jack assured her. "She's going to be my daughter, so they'll accept her too. Straight forward. You'll love mi granddad. Grandma calls him a big lummox at times, and it's often not hard to see why."

"I can't wait," Jenny replied, rubbing her hands and grinning in happy anticipation. "Got me a whole new family."

"Just sorry mi mam can't be here," Jack said quietly, a wistful sigh escaping his lungs. "She loved you, our Jenny, and she would have been chuffed to bits to have you as her daughter-in-law, who lived close enough to see regularly."

"She is, Jack, she is," Jenny replied, drawing him close. "I remember the first time I met her. You took me in when you walked me to my nana's from Woodhouse, that time when I was about seven. She really loved you and would have done anything to make you happy, just as I'm going to do for the rest of your life. I would love to have spent more time with her. She was a lovely, understanding lady, and it's obvious whom you take after."

"I love you, Jenny. I always have," he said, drawing her close. "Why couldn't I have admitted it to myself at the right time? Anyway, enough of that. That was then, and this is now."

He kissed her, feeling her body fitting perfectly next to his, wishing with all his heart that this happiness, this perfection would last forever. He knew it would, because he had known Jenny almost all his life, and he trusted her. Still, he couldn't help but reflect on the perfect marriage he thought he had with Lee.

"Penny?" she said, becoming aware of his quietness and the tight grip he had on her.

He let go quickly, realising he might be hurting her.

"Sorry," he said, stepping back from her. "I hope I didn't hurt you. And please stop calling me Penny."

"Course you didn't, silly," she assured him, laughing at his comment and the slightly confused look in his deep green eyes, "but you were far away."

"Just thinking about Sam," he replied softly. "I know he probably has no idea who I am right now, but I was wondering how he was. As long as he's happy and untroubled and loved, that's all I ask."

"I've never come across any man as unselfish and caring as you, Jack Ingles," she said, in awe of this man who had pledged himself to her unequivocally, and without either reservation or condition. She just couldn't believe her luck. "All I can say is that you won't ever regret coming to me."

"The only regret I have," he went on, shrugging his ample shoulders, "is not coming to you in your time of need five or so years ago. That was the right time."

"But you're here now, and that's all that matters, lovely man," she smiled, snuggling up to him.

"Tea time!" he erupted unexpectedly, making her jump almost out of her skin. "Cup of tea and—"

"A digestive biscuit by any chance?" she added, a smile of familiarity dancing around her mouth. How she had missed him all those years he hadn't been near, and how she had longed for this moment since that day in the churchyard when he had brought joy and hope back into her life.

"No," he replied to a puzzled look on her face. "I have these."

He pulled a confectionery box from the brown carrier bag under the table, out of which he fished, conjurer-like, two … Danish pastries.

"Ooh, goody," she exclaimed, clapping her hands like a child. "Not had those for ages. I'll do the tea."

"Almost mashed," he shouted from the kitchenette. "Just need to get the mugs and plates. On my way through."

"Received this today," she said handing him a letter with a Toronto post-mark, "from the redirection postal service you organised."

"Then why didn't you open it?" he asked, wiping pastry crumbs from his lips and face.

"It's addressed to you," she said, unsure of his response.

"My mail's your mail, my lovely," he answered. "So, open it. I think we know whom it's from, unless we know anyone else living in Canada. It has been three weeks. Thought she'd forgotten me."

"It's from a solicitor," she said, unfolding the single sheet of headed note paper. "You'd better read it."

"Mmm," he muttered, skimming through to get the gist. "She's not contesting, but she does want a fair share of the proceeds from the house we almost bought, and a negotiated amount to pay towards Sam's upkeep. She won't be back."

"Not too bad, I suppose in the circumstances," Jenny shrugged.

"We won't be rolling over on this one, though," he answered. "There is the question of access to my son, which hasn't been addressed, and that needs to be offset against any maintenance payments I might have to make. We'll sort it out, my darling girl. Small price to pay for what I've gained."

He turned to Jenny and gathered her in his arms, kissing

her intently and passionately. She sighed a long, slow sigh of contentment. Her life had changed so radically in a few short weeks that she almost didn't recognise herself. She still lived at 18 Queen Street, but not for much longer. Jack had set up viewings of two or three houses down Ash Gap Lane, Snydale Road, one in the country at Warmfield not far from the Plough, and a couple in Altofts. They were all older houses with character where, co-incidentally, they had both wanted to live.

"They'll be guideline properties," he said, "for us to decide where we would like to live. It's not too far to Leeds, especially when the new motorway comes through. The M62 I think it's to be called. Half an hour into Leeds, or thereabouts."

"They'll need to be exceptional to make me give up the idea of something brand-new and ... big," she warned him. "New stuff and little to do to get what we want."

"Your choice, my sweet," he said, reassuring her that she was in charge. "You'll have to live in it full time until Jessie's a bit older, when you might decide what you would like to do."

"What if I want to have children, stop at home, and bake?" she suggested with a smile. "My scones are—"

"To die for – I know. Then that's what I should like, too," he said honestly. "Whatever you feel comfortable with, you shall do. That won't be my decision. We can afford to live on my salary, but the money your dad left you ... you do with as you wish. I intend to look after my wife and our children. That's what a man's supposed to do, and I'll do it with pride and pleasure."

-o-

"What do you mean, she's taken up with our Jack?" William gasped disbelievingly over breakfast. "He's married to ... whomever. I don't know. I've never met her."

"She told Mum the other day," Val said, matter-of-fact, "and Mum told me."

"But he's not been married two minutes," Willian replied incredulously, "and she's gone off to Canada? With his son? Bad news. Just goes to show you can't trust these colonials."

"I think we ought to visit," Val said, concerned they might be struggling. "We've a week left of our summer break, and I … think we ought to go. There's enough room at Mum's to put us all up."

"Do we have to? Really have to?" William moaned. "I have a lot to do here."

"Like?" she said, a disbelieving frown crossing her brow. "So, what makes this year any different from the ones before it then? He's your brother. Your only brother, for goodness' sake. You stay here if you must, but the rest of us are going. Tomorrow. Our cases are packed, and we're ready to go. Our car's tank is full, and outside our door. Will you miss us?"

"OK. OK," he sighed. "I'll go and pack a bag."

"No need," she smiled triumphantly. "It's done."

The children giggled by the crack in the kitchen door, listening to everything between their mum and dad. The give and take of married life: give by Mum and take – on the chin – by Dad. Funny and entertaining at the same time, it was a comedy show in itself, and Mum always won. Game, set, match … slam dunk.

"Who's driving?" he asked, knowing the answer.

"You are," they all chorused.

He wasn't overly keen on driving all that way, particularly in his tank-like Volvo. Built to keep the little ones safe, the salesman had promised. William hoped he would never have to prove his argument. And it needed its own petrol tanker in tow. Fine for short distances, but the hundred and fifty miles he would need to do to get to Val's mum's in

Cambridge Street wasn't a load of laughs. He couldn't wait to be at the end of the return journey.

"Are we there yet, Daddy?" little Mary asked as they hit the M6 motorway ten minutes after they had set off.

"No, my sweet," he replied, shrugging his shoulders slightly and winking at Val. "Not sure we will even get there. I think we're lost."

The very serious and concerned chorus of "No." and "Can't be." deafened the adults and rocked the car.

"Got you. Got you big style." William guffawed as they sped their usual way to Val's mum's house.

"Daddy?" Mary piped up when it was least expected, as usual.

"Yes, love?" he replied, not surprised to hear her question. Whenever it was likely a child-like question might pop up, she was the one always to ask it. Her brothers were self-sufficient and always within themselves, but little Mary always wanted to know. She possessed an insatiable appetite to know, in her unstoppable quest for knowledge of the world and her place in it.

"I know where we are going," she started, "but what I don't know is why we are going there. Could it be anything to do with our little talk the other day?"

"Talk?" he puzzled. They had so many 'little talks' when they were on their own together.

"You know," she persisted, "the one about Uncle Jack? Has he done something wrong? Only ... I heard you tell Mummy you didn't want to go, and…"

"No, he's not done anything wrong," William said, feeling a little hot under the collar. She was smart and sharp, bringing back memories of the many similar conversations he had had with his brother at the same age.

Val smiled as his little girl made him squirm with discomfort.

"Then," she said, pausing slightly, "why are we going

to see him now? You always tell us a while before we do anything big, but this time you didn't. That's why I thought …

"Mummy? Have you got any of those sucky sweets, please? My ears have just popped, and there's a awful smell in here. Yeeew!"

The younger of the two boys smirked, and his brother, Joey, covered his nose and giggled uncontrollably.

"How many times have I told you," Val turned on the boy, "that if you need to pump, don't do it in the car? Daddy will stop and you can get out."

"It was unexpected, and I couldn't help it," the younger boy sniggered. "It just … came out."

His elder brother buried his face in his jersey front and laughed uncontrollably, all the while trying not to let it show.

"Joey, for goodness' sake grow up," Val told him. "It's a good job you don't live on a farm where the cows do it all the time, only not as smelly as your brother. Open the windows at the back a little, please."

"Are we there yet, Daddy?" Mary's muffled voice piped up after a few moments. "Only … I want to go to the toilet and I need to do a—"

"We don't need details if you don't mind, young lady," Val butted in quickly. "We'll be another five minutes, that's all. Can you hold it until we get to Grandma's?"

"I'll try," Mary said, squirming in the back seat. "I'll … try. I'll really try."

"Little bit quicker, William, if you please," Val urged her husband, "or we might need to change the car."

-o-

Cambridge Street was very quiet for this late in the summer holidays, but then there were never that many children about, even though large family houses lined the streets of this extremely long cul-de-sac. The snicket at the top of the road was wide enough for folks on foot and the occasional bike, but nothing more. These late Edwardian houses, although perhaps slightly past their best, were still impressive and well sought-after – particularly by those who couldn't afford them. Although Val's mum had the family home just as she wanted it, it was no longer a family home, and as such was too big for her own needs. However, those needs did include having enough space to house her daughter's growing brood in relative comfort when they decided to descend upon her for a few days.

She loved having her family come to stay. It was the only time this grand old house rang to the sound of children's laughter and to hurrying, scurrying feet – happy sounds she couldn't get enough of. She missed her husband dreadfully, too. There were times when he had been boorishly overbearing, but he had loved his home, and he had doted on his girls. She missed his half-smiling half-solemn face at the breakfast table as he ate his toast in the same way every morning, and that space that held his warm body next to her in bed was now empty and cold.

"Goodness," she said as the children poured through the door. "Look at you all! You've all grown so big. Mary, how—"

"Sorry, Nana," Mary gasped as she shot past. "I need the toilet to do a…"

"Mary," Val urged. "No details. Just go."

"Are you sure you're OK with us here for a few days?" William asked Mrs McDermot. "Only—"

"We need to be here, William," Val interrupted sternly, eyes flashing. "It's your brother and my sister we're talking about. If Jenny and Jack aren't important to you, they are to me."

"As long as you need, William," Mrs McDermot assured him. "As long as you need."

William wasn't convinced they needed to be there at all, but his wife had insisted, and he liked an easy life. So, who was he to argue? He hadn't seen his brother in quite a while, and, truth be known, he hadn't missed him. He had his busy successful life to lead and he didn't need constant reminders of his inadequacies compared with his brother. Jack, on the other hand, had always looked up to his brother, always feeling he didn't see him enough. Jack had never spent much time with William because of age and distance issues, but he had wanted to redress that imbalance at the first opportunity.

"Look after the children, Mum, will you please, while we go to see Jenny?" Val asked. "They might need something to drink and eat. OK?"

"Of course it is, dear," she replied. "But why do you need to go to see your sister so soon? Won't it wait until tomorrow? You've only just got here."

"No, Mum," Val replied pointedly, "it won't wait. William?"

"Car?" he asked, as they walked down the front path.

"Car?" she replied incredulously. "It's only ten minutes' walk. Remember? Queen Street? Come on."

She flung the gate wide and marched off down the road towards Church Lane, William trailing in her wake, trying valiantly to catch up.

"Val," he called. "Val!"

She stopped and turned around, an impatient and irritated look on her face.

"Wait for me, please?" he shouted. "Why the hurry? Shall we get there together? Or do you want to control what will be said and done?"

"I'm sorry, love," she said quietly, linking his arm with hers as he drew near. "I want to sort things out with them. That's all."

"Who was it said they were both important to her?"

William reminded her. "Oh, yes. It was you. If there's anything wants sorting out, they'll be the ones to do it. Don't you think?"

"I suppose so," she agreed, "but I just wanted to hear it from them."

"Hello, Jenny," Val started, as the door to number 18 Queen Street opened slowly. "Hello, Jack."

"'Ey up, Jenny," Jack called, as she let them in. "Storm troopers have arrived. As if we didn't know why they're here."

"Now just a minute," William interrupted, raising his voice slightly. "We—"

"Don't you 'just a minute' us," Jack retaliated sharply. "We know why you're here, and—"

"Let them say what they have to say, Jack," Jenny said quietly. "You never know, they might want to hear what we have to say, too."

"Cup of tea and a digestive or two?" Jack offered, his tone becoming pragmatically more friendly. "We might as well try to keep the terms of engagement at least a little cordial. After all, we are family."

"Jack," Jenny said, a slight smile creeping to her mouth corners. "Come in then, you two. Sitting? Or is this to be a formal gathering rather than a nice family reunion?"

There was going to be neither admonitory tone nor moralising here, as Jenny and Jack were determined to follow their jointly chosen path. Besides, who were Val and William to tell them what was good and not good to do with their lives?

"We are only concerned about you both," Val replied, casting a furtive glance at her husband, seeking his support.

"And why should you be ... 'concerned'?" Jack asked, pointedly. "Do we look as if we need looking after? Is there something we've done wrong? Don't forget that Jenny's husband walked out, and my wife took my son off to

Canada having encouraged me to spend a few quality days with Jud and Marion. Devious or what?"

Jenny set the tray of crockery and tea pot on the little table under the window, ready to pour when it was mashed.

"Any chance she'll return?" William asked, subdued and sorry he had doubted.

"On a scale of one to ten?" Jack said. "Minus two. She'd obviously been planning her move for some time with her father, as he's been backwards and forwards to Canada several times over the last six months or so. Got me out of the way for a few days and then – bingo."

"But why?" Val asked, puzzled that anyone could behave like that.

"Brainwashed by him, and totally under his control," Jack replied, leaning back in his chair with a sigh. "There have been signs over the months that I've not picked up on, until too late."

"And now?" William said, shuffling uncomfortably in his chair. "You know…"

"You mean us living together like man and wife, William," Jenny said pointedly, "and everything that means?"

William blushed and nodded briefly, not wishing to pursue the question of their relationship any further.

"I love Jenny completely," Jack explained, "and always have. It has taken this fiasco for me to realise that, and to understand this is where I should have been from the start. Not ideal, but it's a new beginning for us."

"And the freedom to marry?" Val asked. "I assume you want to marry … eventually?"

"Of course we do," Jack insisted, a surprised grin splitting his face. "We want to have children together, and, to do that, we need to be married. Divorce papers have been served, and, according to my brief, it shouldn't be too long. Anyway, Jess needs a father, and I have decided – we have decided – that I will adopt her as my own."

William and Val threw hurried, surprised glances at each other as they tried to come to terms with this heap of stuff they had never encountered before.

"So, you've thought it through, then?" William asked lamely.

"Of course we have," Jack replied forcefully. "Come on, William. When did you ever know me not to think things through before acting? I've always been here to decide on stuff, whereas other folks never have."

Jenny looked at her magnificent Jack, recognising the signs that something significant had been bothering him. She knew that he alone was the man she needed and wanted, but wondered what he was about to say that had obviously been turning around in his mind.

"And by that you mean—?" William asked.

Snap! The trap had been sprung.

"Well, William," Jack began, allowing his resentment towards his brother to trickle out. "Where do I start?"

Once his controlled outpouring of upset around his brother's lack of concern for his mam's feelings surrounding his distance had reached their logical and pragmatic conclusion, there remained an uncomfortable silence swirling around his brother and his wife. They both knew Jack was right, and they accepted individually the upset their lack of thought and compassion for others must have caused. They had been so wrapped up in their own cycle of work-children-work that they hadn't spared a thought for those dear to them outside of that circle. Val was as guilty of this with her own close family, as was William with his. Her dad had died when she wasn't there, and she hadn't seen him for months before his funeral.

Tears began to well in her eyes as William slid his arm around her shoulders. Not ones to express feelings publicly, their pleading eyes reached out to Jack and Jenny.

"No animosity, Bro," Jack said, recalling William's time in the army, "but it had to be said. I don't want you to make the same mistake when your little 'uns are grown up. It's just that mi mam couldn't understand why you rarely came, and although she never said, I knew what she was feeling."

William smiled at the army reference, realising ruefully that he had once again learned a sharp lesson from his younger but much wiser brother.

"What now with you two, then?" Val asked.

"It's all sorted," Jack replied. "Things will now take their course."

"Why did I know you'd say that?" William laughed, his gloom beginning to dispel.

"We'll live together here until we find a place of our own," Jenny cut in, "as our own little family. That reminds me … Jessie's asleep upstairs, and I need to see to her."

"We'll have to go as well," Val said, getting up from the settee. "Mum can cope with our three only for so long. Coming back with us?"

"No, if it's all right with you," Jack replied. "Later, perhaps, if you're still here."

"We're staying a couple of nights," his brother chipped in.

"Later, then," Jack said, as they opened the door, "and thanks for dropping by."

The door clicked shut as a smile of satisfied triumph crossed Jack's face. He didn't want to fall out with his brother, but there had been issues festering in his mind that needed to be laid to rest. Now William had no illusions about his 'little' brother's views and his ability and will to share them. He loved his brother, and had always had the utmost regard and respect for him as a sibling and a man. However, he had been lacking in certain areas of humanity for too long. Hopefully now he would be reminded of the importance of his responsibilities towards all his family members.

"Was I a little too pointed there, do you think, Jenny?" Jack asked as she came back into the room with little Jessie in tow. "Only, it's been on my mind since before mi mam died."

"You were calm, authoritative, and you articulated your thoughts and feelings amazingly well, my lovely man," she reassured him, snuggling up to him on the settee. "You could have been firmer, but you didn't need to be, so I don't think there'll be any issue about you and me from now on."

"Do you know what I'd like to do day after tomorrow?" Jack asked her, pulling her closer.

"No," she laughed, "but I should think you're about to tell me."

"I'd like to go and see my cousin, Irene, and my pal, David, in Leeds," he said, a half-smile on his lips. "I think I've told you about them before, haven't I? I need to tell them about the situation with Lee, and of course to show you off as the love of my life."

"You have, briefly," she answered, "and that would be an excellent idea. I should love to meet them. Love of your life, eh? I like that, but make it the love of both our lives."

Chapter 10

"David," Irene yelled from the top of the stairs. "There's someone at the front door. David!"

"Got it, my beloved pixie," he shouted back, a huge Cheshire grin joining his ears. "Almost there. "Who on earth could—?"

He loved his life with this gorgeous creature, and he had his pal Jack to thank, which he did virtually every day. They hadn't seen him or Lee since Jack had moved in to the rarefied atmosphere of secondary education, and he had wondered why. David and Irene didn't even know where their friends lived.

"Hello. Good morning, young lady," David gushed as he opened the door. "What can I do you for on this lovely rainy day?"

"Mr Aston? Mr David Aston?" the young lady replied. "Is Irene in?"

"Does she owe you money?" he quipped, a great smile adorning his face. "And if she doesn't, who should I say wants her?"

"It's Jenny," she said. "Jenny McDermot."

He turned back into the hall, pulling the door to as he shouted for his wife. When he turned back…

"Hello, David," a familiar voice attacked him from behind. "Long time no see."

"Jack," David grinned. "You old son of a gun. Nice trick,

but it didn't have me fooled for an instant though, old chap."

"Yeah, right," Jack guffawed. "Who are you trying to kid? Not going to ask us in?"

"Of course I am," he said, wringing Jack's hand hard enough to pull it off. "Not going to introduce me to this gorgeous young lady?"

"When we're inside," Jack replied quietly, "if that's all right with you? And where's my favourite cousin?"

"I'm here," Irene gushed, taking hold of him in a warm hug of where-have-you-been sort of love.

"And this is Jenny," Jack said calmly and slowly, "whom I have known all my life and who is, and always has been … the love of my life."

"But—" Irene stuttered, as she threw a puzzled look towards David.

"Before we explain," Jack butted in politely, "any chance of—?"

"A cup of tea and a digestive?" Irene grinned, her mind chasing back to that first meeting with her Auntie Flo, which at times seemed like only yesterday. "Of course there is. I'm sorry for my lack of manners."

"May I come and help?" Jenny offered quietly, as Irene made for the kitchen.

"Of course you may," Irene replied with a smile. "It won't take long, and then we can begin to fill in the missing details."

"This is a lovely house," Jenny said as she waited for her tea to cool enough to drink. "Makes mine look and feel like a shoe box."

"Fortunately," David added, "Mother decided the family home was growing beyond her needs, and so we all agreed she would allow us to have this one, and we would buy her one of the new mews houses they've just built in Farthing Lane a couple of streets from here. It has new everything and a manageable back garden she can enjoy. Win-win for us – for now."

"And you have a new daughter, I believe," Jack said, a smile growing. "You always said I could be godfather, if you remember, David?"

"Post's still open, old man," David agreed eagerly. "We were holding off on the official christening until you resurfaced – and we knew you would. She's called Jessica."

"Snap!" Jenny and Jack laughed in unison. "Same here."

"But," Irene frowned, thrown by this revelation. "I thought yours was a boy called Sam?"

Jack's cue to start the saga of deceit and betrayal had just been given.

They sat in absolute, stunned silence while Jack regaled them with events leading up to their being before them this minute.

"Still haven't had an explanation why she left, or why she took my lad away from me," Jack said. "Jenny is the one I should have married a long time ago, but that mistake will be rectified just as soon as the decrees come through. Who'd have thought it, eh? Both deserted."

"I can't believe she was so deceitful, to encourage you to spend time with your folks while she was planning the Great Escape with, of all people, her father," Irene gasped, putting her arm around his shoulders.

"How can she be allowed to get away with stealing your son from you?" David said, the closest thing to anger growing in his eyes. "Can't you—?"

"She's in Canada, David," Jack replied, pragmatic to the last, "over three thousand miles yonder, t'other side o' yon big puddle. Besides, as long as he's looked after and happy, my feelings count as nought. My responsibilities lie here with Jenny and—"

"Jessica!" David and Irene chorused. "Just twigged why you both said 'snap'. Coincidence, eh?"

"And you two have known each other—?" Irene asked.

"More than twenty years," Jack replied. "Since we were in Mrs Gunn's class at Woodhouse Junior School. My brother married Jenny's sister, Val."

"Bit of a long way to travel to work, don't you think, old chap?" David said scratching his head. "I mean, Normanton to Leeds?"

"I used to do it every day as a student teacher," Jack said, "and by bus, train, and bus. Too soft and privileged you, David, living on the door step."

"Try the Outback," Irene butted in. "That's what you call tough."

"A bit like living on Queen Street in our town then," Jack chipped in to huge guffaws from Jenny. "Still, we will look at moving – perhaps to Leeds when the dust has settled. We might even come and live next to you. That'll bring the tone and value of your property down, eh?"

"Oh, no," David groaned in mock shock. "Your gardening skills would show me up."

"Gardening?" Jenny huffed. "Since when did you ever grow anything?"

"Since Percy Thrower were a lad," Jack laughed. "I used to like rhubarb out of mi mam's back garden at Garth Avenue. It was the onny thing mi father did rayt. Oh, and eggs from his chickens when he first tried his hand at having an allotment."

"That's something you never told me about," Irene said.

"It was all right," Jack went on, "until he tried to charge mi mam for 'em. She told him where he could lay 'em in no uncertain terms."

"No home-grown eggs after that, then?" David said with a grin.

"Not really," Jack added. "It wasn't long after that as 'e took up wi' Dotty French again, and I'm pretty sure I know where his eggs were laid after that."

"And your Jessica?" David asked.

"Jessie's with my mother," Jenny replied, "keeping her company. Since my dad passed away, it's been a lifesaver for her. She does try to tell me how to raise her, naturally, but she is my daughter – and soon to be Jack's – so Mum accepts, reluctantly at times, that she is ours to bring up."

"Jack's?" Irene puzzled. "Is she his, as in … his?"

"Biologically, no," Jack interrupted, "but since the father doesn't even want to know her, we thought we would give her a proper dad, through adoption."

"Wow," David exhaled loudly. "An instant dad."

"Not really," Jack said, a little taken aback by his tone. "It's going to take a while because of the divorces, and we need to try to find the man to tell him what's happening. The way I look at it is this: Jessie should have been my daughter, had I done the right thing to start with. Can't cry ower spilt Tetleys, so we're going to put it right as soon as we can."

Irene smiled. She knew Jack would have it all thought through. He wouldn't be able to live with himself if he didn't put right in his own mind what he had caused to be wrong. She had learned that much about her cousin. He could be stubborn at times, but, when it came to rationalising difficult situations, Jack never baulked at doing what was fair and just. How well her Auntie Flo had known him. She was probably the only one in the world who understood and accepted all his foibles. She couldn't imagine how much he missed her. She missed her mother, but she hadn't been anywhere near as tight as Jack and his mam.

"Any news from Broughton, then?" Jack asked politely, not really too interested, knowing full well that the status quo would never change much. No doubt Cecil P Barchester would have made some changes and certain improvements, but the basic infrastructure in the new building would have remained the same.

"Well," David started, "Barchester has made something

of a difference to how the school functions. Nothing's haphazard or left to chance anymore. Planning's so good and, for example, the role of deputy has become so demanding that Sparks couldn't take any more on his lop-sided shoulders."

"And?" Jack asked in anticipation.

"He's retired with effect from … now," David smiled, leaning back on his chair, a self-satisfied smile creasing his eye corners.

"Don't tell me," Jack said, a wicked grin creeping up on him. "He's appointed my good friend … Vanessa?"

"Nooo," David hooted, realising almost immediately that his pal was taking a rise out of him. "Me."

"I was joking, of course, old man," Jack laughed, shaking his hand and giving him a congratulatory slap on the back. "Congratulations. Couldn't have gone to a better man. From when?"

"One week and three days will see me in the hot seat vacated by Sparks," David replied, beaming his satisfaction to the world. "Well, luke-warm seat at best."

"You'll absolutely love it," Jack observed, "lording it over everybody. How has Stanley taken it, your leap-frogging over his more than ample back?"

"A bit stand-offish at first, because he applied for the job as well," David said, "but when Barchester explained to him what was involved and expected, and that it needed a younger – and better – man—"

"David…" Irene butted in, a little frown underlining her shock at his unkindness towards his colleague.

"It's OK, Rene," Jack assured her with a huge grin. "He doesn't mean it. Always been a running joke between the three of us. David's better at one or two things, and Stanley is better at everything else."

"Cheers, pal," David said, a smile growing. "I'll do the same for you one of these days. Is that Lee's Mini I see…?"

"My Mini," Jack insisted. "It's the only thing I came away with from this total fiasco, and that's dropping to bits. Probably need to change it for an MGB. I've always liked them."

"An MGB?" Jenny turned swiftly around, a look of concern tiptoeing across her face. "I thought—?"

"Sorry, love," Jack grinned sheepishly as he slid his arm around her waist. "My sense of humour. I only said it because I hate 'em. Our growing family wouldn't fit into a shoe box like that. We need something more substantial … something like a Cortina or a Cavalier."

"Growing family?" Irene queried, guessing but not sure.

"We would soon like to be pregnant," Jenny announced with pride, as she snuggled closer to Jack, and he drew her to him.

"But—?" David said, becoming increasingly puzzled at this 'new' union that pre-dated all others.

"Sometimes speed is important," Jack said, "to make up for lost time. We want a family that comes from both of us too. Jessie will be loved as if she came from us both, no differently from any of our issue."

"Have you found somewhere to accommodate all the children you might have?" Irene asked, genuinely concerned that they might be in too much of a hurry to perpetuate their line. "You always considered it would be marriage before sex, though, didn't you?"

"True," he replied, "and look where that got me. We will be together 'until death us do—' That we know. Always did. One day."

"We're looking at houses Warmfield way on," Jenny said, happy to share their good news.

"Within striking distance of both the Pineapple and the Plough," Jack added. "My old stamping ground. Had many a rousing session in the Plough over a bottle or two of Newcastle Brown on a Saturday night, after a day's rugby beating every team in Yorkshire."

"Bit of an exaggeration, old boy?" David said, a disbelievingly indulgent smile creeping across his face.

"Tell that to Messrs Jubb, Moreton and Whale," Jack scoffed at his disbelief, "the teachers involved with our rugby teams. At the risk of repeating myself, and becoming a bore, we were proud of the fact that we didn't lose a First XV match when I was in the sixth form, and QEGS Wakefield refused us a first team game after we stuffed their second team twenty-five nil."

"You?" Irene laughed. "Repeating yourself? Never."

They all burst out laughing at Irene's funny, and the face Jack pulled at it.

"You are staying for one of Irene's legendary hot pots, aren't you?" David said, to enthusiastic nods from his wife. "And then staying the night?"

"We hadn't planned to," Jack said, "but seeing as you insist, it would be rude to refuse."

"Excellent," David replied, a satisfied grin spreading across his face. "This needs to happen more often. I need all the friends I can get, especially from September."

"Pregnant?" Jack asked in bed that night. "Already?"

"I don't know," Jenny answered, snuggling closer to his warm body. "I just feel that it's about right to be expecting."

"All the more reason why we need to have that house up Warmfield way," he said, drawing her to him. "Should we take ... precautions?"

"No," she giggled quietly. "It's time, Jack. It's time."

Their love-making was slow, gentle, and easy, and they delighted in what they felt they would achieve. This was not only for them, it was for their family.

"Are we ready for a new baby?" David asked his wife quietly, as he slid into his side of the bed next to her. "I mean—"

"I think we are, my lover," she whispered. "Your new job

says we can afford it, and I think little Jessica will need a brother, or maybe even two."

David's grin, as he turned out the light, hinted his agreement to her.

Chapter 11

October that year was gloriously warm and uncharacteristically sunny, following the Indian summer to end all summers. So little rain had blighted their early autumn that calls for a hosepipe ban had surfaced to spoil their fun. Haw Hill park had clasped the summer flowers planted in early May to its bosom, not wishing to let them go just yet.

Sadly, however, Jack's granddad's condition had deteriorated, confining him temporarily to a bed at Clayton Hospital while his doctors puzzled over the right approach to halt his decline. Consequently, Jack became the self-appointed chauffeur for his grandma's evening visits to see him. Although they tried valiantly to lift his spirits, he knew that Black Lung was beginning to reel him in, leaving him ultimately no escape.

"Int it time tha were out o' this place, Owd Man?" Jack would say to him. "Tha can't surely like yon 'ospital food so much tha can't drag thissen away from it, can tha?"

"Nay, lad," he would reply, "I don't like being 'ere any more than thy likes comin' to see me like this, but them there medics seem to be at a loss as to what to do wi' me. Inevitable, really. There's onny one outcome, and we'll have to face it when it raises its 'ead. None of us'll last forever."

Marion would sit by, quietly listening to the dire words she didn't want to hear, that her Jud was all but giving up hope for any future. They'd been together through good and bad times for more than fifty years, and she had wanted it to be many more. He had been her rock, and she didn't know how she would cope without him. He was annoying at times, but she did love the big lummox of a man, who worshipped the ground she stepped on.

That first visit hadn't sat well with Jack. It was hard to see his granddad in such a poorly state, reduced to a shadow of his former self – a towering man both physically and mentally. He vowed he couldn't do it again, but he knew he would, because each time might be the last, and he couldn't live with himself if he missed it. It was his granddad, for goodness' sake, and he had played a big part in making him the man he had turned out to be.

"You all right, love?" Jenny asked over tea. Although her mother had said otherwise, she was a very good cook: nothing fancy, but just the sort of food he adored.

"Sorry, what d'you say?" he replied, jerking out of his deep reverie, not having heard a word she'd said.

"You were a universe away," she smiled, ever conscious there were worlds rushing about in his head that she could only imagine.

"Bit concerned about mi granddad," he said quietly, dropping back briefly into the hospital ward. "I think he's fading, and I wish I could stop the slide."

"I know what you mean," she answered, taking his hand gently in hers. "You feel so … helpless, and not in control. For you, my lovely, that must be doubly hard."

"He's the only real father I've known," Jack said, tears welling in his eyes, "and I've learned such a lot from him. I don't want to lose him, Jenny."

"What can I say?" she answered after an awkward pause. "You'll just have to enjoy him while he's still with you. Can we come visit when you next go?"

"We?" he said, puzzled at the reference. There was only

one 'we' in his life.

"Me and our Jessie," she said, quite matter-of-fact. "We are part of your life, and – by association – part of his, too."

Her logic left him gasping at times, and as such couldn't be faulted. Consequently, he couldn't refuse.

"Put like that," he said, "the answer has to be 'yes'. Thank you."

"What for?" she puzzled, brows drawing her forehead down. "I'm only thinking the sort of logic you would use. What do you call it? Pragmatic."

"The two most important people in mi life up to being with you," he said slowly, dropping to a whispered rasp, "gone within four or five years of each other."

"You can't say that, love," she said quietly, putting her arms around him. "Your granddad's still here."

"Onny just," he insisted, clearly upset at what he saw as the end of a significant chapter in his life. Deep in his own turmoil, he hadn't spared a single thought as to how Jud's demise would affect his grandma. She was a dour, hard-faced Yorkshire lass who seemed on the surface to be able to cope with everything life threw at her. She had had a few googlies bowled at her in her time, and had batted them away to the boundary seemingly with consummate ease.

To those who knew her, however, the inner turmoil had all but consumed her, her beloved Herbert at twenty-four, and then her equally loved son, Jack, at twenty-two. How would she cope with losing Jud, the man who had supported her and loved her throughout all her trials?

Jack's traipsing backwards and forwards to his job in Leeds had allowed tiredness to creep upon him. He couldn't, however, let his grandma down. She relied on him to help her spend her husband's last weeks with him as he slipped slowly away from them, uncertain what was taking him away.

"He's not long for this world, Jen," Jack said, hugging

and kissing her and Jessie as he came in late from his visit to Clayton Hospital with his grandma. A tear began to well and threaten, as thoughts of his mam flooded into his already sad mind. He didn't want a replay of the anguish and emotional wrench he had experienced with her. It was important he learn to prepare for the inevitable.

His granddad had been an incredibly important part of his existence, both growing up and as a man, and it creased him to watch Jud step slowly out of his physical life.

"Then we all must be there for him," Jenny replied, hugging Jack, "and for your grandma. We mustn't forget her, because she will have to carry on when he's gone. At her age, she can't be left to fend for herself. Our Val and your William can't be relied on. They've got other priorities that don't understand all this 'poorly' business."

-o-

"…And your translation of the exam questions into and from French has to be both accurate and idiomatically correct," Jack explained to his A level French group. "However—"

"Mr Ingles," a quietly authoritative voice crept into his explanation from the doorway to his classroom, "may I have a word, please?"

"Certainly, Headmaster," Jack said, turning towards the source of the voice. "OK, chaps, turn to your critiques and plan your next moves."

He followed Mr Matthews out, once he had settled his students to their tasks.

"Have you had a letter from the education office, inviting you for interview?" the head asked quietly.

"Interview?" Jack said, perplexed at such a strange question. "Interview for where?"

"For Merton Grange School," the head continued. "A newly-established middle school in North-East Leeds."

"I applied, as I told you, a while ago," Jack explained, "but I never heard anything. Thought I hadn't been considered. Why?"

"Well," the head continued, "you have an interview today, in half an hour."

"Half an hour?" Jack replied, shocked. "Where?"

"The education office, of course," Mr Matthews said. "Great George Street in Leeds."

"Then I can't go," Jack said, a sigh betraying his disappointment. "No time to get there – and if there were, nowhere to park."

"I've arranged for the caretaker to take you in his car. He will drop you off outside the offices, so off to the washroom to freshen up – chalk off hands and so on – and then, good luck. I'll see you when you get back."

With that he ushered Jack away, and slipped into his classroom to continue with Jack's lesson.

Stunned, and now not so confident, he rushed out to Mr James the caretaker, who was sitting in his Hillman Imp, engine humming peacefully.

"OK, Jack?" Mr James asked.

"OK, Harry," Jack replied. "On our way, and don't spare the horse power, eh?"

At five to eleven in the morning, Leeds was busy. The Woodhouse Lane road past Lewis's and on to the Headrow was always nose to tail no matter what time of day, and Cookridge Street north to Great George Street similarly. Good driver that he was, Harry James had Jack outside the education offices only five minutes after his interview start time. His last "Good luck, mate" left Jack on the pavement, contemplating the edifice before him – only the first time since the start of his career on leaving college. It hadn't changed – either outside or in.

The same dour, unprepossessing exterior tricked you into the same quaint if musty-smelling inside.

Although noticed and noted, the inside décor was irrelevant. The inbuilt discomfort of those leatherette straight-backed chairs was designed to keep interviewees awake and alert before their ordeal. Deliberate or accidental, the reasoning had become lost over time.

There was no need for excuse and apology for his lateness, because they already knew, and wanted solely to focus on experience and ability. Jack's interview, the last for this particular job, stretched to a shade over twenty minutes, seemed to be inconsequential in content and purpose, and gave the impression that the outcome had already been decided.

"Mr Ingles?" the prospective head teacher of the new school called to Jack, as the group of four hopefuls awaited its fate.

"Yes, Mr Byrne," he replied, rising automatically from his discomfort.

"May we speak to you, please?" the head said, ushering him back into the grilling room, the traditional way of letting him know that the job was his – if he wanted it.

The late autumn sun winked through the light cloud, casting weak shadows as Jack emerged from perhaps the shortest interview process on record. Virtually shell-shocked by the less-than-memorable occasion, he ambled unsteadily to the top of Cookridge Street, by the Art College, from where a number one Lawnswood bus – a route he had travelled many times in his student days – would chauffeur him to within a short walk from school on the Ring Road.

The bell for the start of last lesson – a free period for Jack – had barely stopped vibrating as he walked into the head's office to tell him the news. Mr Matthews was disappointed but, recognising Jack's worth, he knew he wouldn't be able to keep him because he didn't have the scope to promote. His loss was someone else's gain, unfortunately ... a loss he hoped he would fill, but doubted it would happen in the short term. Fortunately for him, Jack would be with him until the end of this academic year – next July.

By the time he was in the car ready for home, he was becoming light-headed and dying to feel food in his belly and hot tea down his throat. The most trying and testing part of the day had been missing his lunch and afternoon tea. Although he knew traffic bottlenecks on Vicar Lane and Crown Point Road out of Leeds would be stiff at this time of day, he always enjoyed watching the magnificent horse-drawn brewery drays loading barrels in Tetley's yard on Black Bull Street.

Once the John O' Gaunt pub on Leeds Road was in his rear-view mirror, he knew he was on his home run.

"You look tired, love," Jenny said after kissing and hugging her man, once the door had been shut. "Busy day?"

"You could say that," he replied, launching in to the tale of his day, "and it means from next September we will have quite a bit more money to play with. Consequently, we need to start our house-hunting in earnest."

"You clever, smart man," she whooped, flinging herself at him.

"Slow down. Slow down," he grinned. "Now I know you are only with me because of my money."

They laughed happily together, talking about what this promotion would do for them and their family prospects.

"I've a bit of OK news for you too, my lovely," Jenny said as they sat down with their usual cup of tea.

"Go on, then," Jack urged her. "What could be better news than we won't be strapped for cash anymore? Well?"

"Well," Jenny said slowly, making him wait, and choosing her time carefully, "I think I've found us a house."

"Really?" he said, a smile growing. "Come on. Tell me more. How did you do that?"

"I borrowed Dad's car, that Mum doesn't like or use,"

she started, "and decided to have a drive around the areas we said we liked."

"Drive? You?" he puzzled. "But I didn't know—"

"That I could drive?" she smiled. "Passed my test when I was just eighteen."

"Wow!" he whistled softly. "'Ark at you ... smarty pants. Anyway – our new house?"

"Up Wakefield Road, towards Warmfield," she said, a self-satisfied smile nestling on her face. "You know? Those nice semis we've always liked? On the left-hand side as you go on towards the new road? Right at the end."

"Fantastic!" he gushed. "But we'll never be able to afford one of them."

"Just over four grand?" she said quietly, her eyes never leaving his face. "Three bedrooms. Just big enough for the four of us – for now."

"Yes," he replied, punching the air. "Hang on ... the four of us?"

"Jessie's going to have a baby brother – or sister," she went, on matter-of-fact, just as he was sucking the chocolate from his digestive. The effect of that piece of news was volcanic. He turned crimson rapidly, descending into a bout of coughing as a piece of biscuit lodged firmly in his wind pipe.

"You're pregnant?" he gasped, once the last crumb had shot out of his mouth. "But ... how...?"

"I think you know how, Jack," Jenny burst out laughing. "At least, I hope you know how."

He picked her up and danced around the floor with her, smothering her face in kisses as he did so. He stopped abruptly mid-jig, and pulled her closer to him, his body heaving gently against hers as tears began to roll down his cheeks.

"Jack?" she said, concerned at his reaction. "You are pleased? Aren't you?"

"Course I am," he insisted, wiping his face on her jumper shoulder. "Why wouldn't I be? I'm ecstatic, but I was just thinking about mi mam – and your dad, of course – who would have loved to have been here to see, and to share."

They sat quietly on the settee in each other's arms, sharing this divine moment of family peace that both had wanted for such a long time.

"We'd better shape ourselves," Jack said as he got up. "Time to pick up mi grandma to visit t'Owd Man."

"We'll have tea when we get back," she replied. "Perhaps we might catch our 'new house' on the way."

"I like the sound of that," he agreed, as he slipped his coat back on, and started the car again.

There was a searching chill to the early evening that didn't sit very well with Jenny. A definite heat lover, she shrank back into herself at any hint of cold, and didn't really relax until summer's promise of warmer weather hopped around the corner. The time taken to his grandma's was so short you could have held your breath for the duration.

"Strange," he muttered, as they walked down the path to the side door.

"What is?" Jenny asked. "No light on?"

"Mmm," he murmured as he rattled the door and walked around to the back. "She's not in, you know. Wonder why?"

"Do you think she's forgotten we were coming for her?" Jenny ventured. "She is getting on a bit, you know."

"Hello ... Jack?" a shrill voice joined them at the back of the house.

Jack swung around to see Mrs Churchill at number thirty-nine, peering over the dividing fence.

"She's gone to t'hospital," Mrs Churchill went on. "Your granddad's taken a turn for t'worse, so she asked me to tell you when you got here."

"How did she get there?" he asked, puzzled.

"Jud's nephew, Harry Burton, took her," Mrs Churchill

replied. "You know? The one from the bread shop opposite the Empire? She said it were urgent you got to know as soon as you got here."

Jack turned to Jenny, a look of panic in his eyes. He grabbed her hand and headed to the car as quickly as he could. That same feeling of foreboding he had experienced before his mam's death began to invade his senses now. What if…?

The journey to Clayton Hospital shot by in a blur, but seemed to take an age, when the only thing that kept him on this earth was Jenny's hand on his thigh, steadying him, letting him know she was there.

"Mummy?" a tiny, tinny voice piped up from the rear of the car.

"Yes, love? What is it?" Jenny answered, turning around to attend to Jessie.

"Why Daddy sad?" her little voice puzzled.

"Well," Jenny started, not one to tell an untruth to her child, "we're going to visit Granddad in hospital, and he's a bit poorly. OK?"

The car park at the hospital was full as usual at this hour – the main visiting time. Smiling faces, arms full with flowers, grapes and many more goodies, passed the time with other smiling faces as they ambled into the building; happy for some, forbidding and fraught for others.

The glass tunnel linking reception with wards and theatres funnelled them into the bowels of the building, where bodies were patched for this world, or dispatched to the next.

"Grandma?" Jack said, surprised to see her sitting in the waiting area, her head in her hands, sobbing. It wasn't like her to make a public show of emotion or its release. His heart sank as he rushed to her, experiencing feelings close to those that washed over him when his mam died. "What is it?"

"He's gone, lad," she sobbed, bereft. "He's gone."

"Stay with her, Jenny, please," he pleaded, "while I find out what's happened."

"Cardiac arrest, Mr Ingles," the nurse's voice echoed quietly in his non-responding brain. "His heart simply stopped beating."

No! What are you saying? This can't be happening. No ... not again.

"And we found him in the early hours. Nothing we could do, I'm afraid. I'm very sorry for your loss."

He turned, tears welling in his eyes, and all he could see were the gently heaving shoulders of his distraught grandmother, trying to come to terms with this inevitable but devastating reality.

Chapter 12

"Granddad's dead, William," Jack urged on the phone, becoming increasingly irate at his brother's intransigence. "You have to find the time. Grandma's distraught, and t'funeral's a week tomorrow. You're allowed time off for funerals and such like. I know you are. The children need to come, too. It's our only granddad and their only great granddad for God's sake!"

It was obvious he wasn't getting anywhere, and that he would have to arrange things himself. That he could do very easily, but his brother should have been the first to put his hand up. This dragged deep, bitter feelings to the surface again of how William had dealt with his mam's funeral. These were feelings he had wanted to remain buried, and hadn't wanted to share, even at their last airing with his brother and sister-in-law. Not now. Not ever.

The telephone receiver rattled alarmingly as its Bakelite frame hit its base, and threatened to shatter on to the floor.

Although Jack remained tight-lipped, Jenny knew he was angry. She touched his hand, which still gripped the little phone table, as he searched desperately for a solution and for control.

"He's not coming, is he?" she said quietly, stroking his skin, trying to soothe. She had learned at times like this to support but not to intrude too deeply into his thoughts. Her Jack had to sort things out in his own mind before acting, as had always been the case. He would never say nor do anything until all was entirely straight in his head. Once he knew, he acted quickly.

"No, he's not," Jack replied quietly. "I know he's got other things on. But … Granddad, for goodness' sake? There have been lots of things in our lives we wouldn't have done without Granddad's intervention. I'm just so sad I couldn't have been there, and I'm even more saddened because he is finding excuses not to come."

He turned and buried his head in Jenny's embrace as they slumped on to the settee. He gave way to emotion rarely, but he was very close now as the recent hurt oozed to the surface and tried to drown him.

Seeing him saddened like this, she decided to phone her sister to see if she had enough sway over her husband to persuade him to change his mind. Meanwhile, he had to decide what to do about his grandma, not knowing how she would react to life without the undoubted rock in her life.

"You all right, my lovely?" Jenny asked, kissing Jack's spikes as he straightened himself next to her.

"Not really," he replied with a heart-felt sigh. "I'm tired of people not doing what they should be doing, and lying about why they're not doing it. Why can't everybody be straight and truthful? It wouldn't hurt them, would it? I can't cope with all this subterfuge and these mealy-mouthed falsehoods that we seem to be surrounded by these days."

"You're too good, honest and straight, my beautiful man," Jenny said to him, holding him close to her, afraid to let him go in case he vanished in a puff of air.

"We'll manage, as we always do," she said, "despite the spanners people are trying to throw into the works. What are we going to do about Marion? We can't just leave her to fend for herself."

"We'll have to keep a close eye on her," he replied,

"and make sure nothing untoward happens. She needs our support now more than ever, but the one thing we mustn't do is to let these 'problems' deflect us from our path."

"Jenny, love? Jack?" a familiar voice crept in through the inner porch. "You there?"

"Through here, Mum," Jenny replied. "In the front room."

"Just had a strange telephone call from our Val," Mrs McDermot started, a concerned frown hovering on her brow.

"Strange," Jenny replied as her mum sat at the table, ready for a cup of tea. "Jack's just come off the phone with his brother."

"Well," Mrs McDermot went on, "she says William walked out the day before, and she's not heard from him since."

"Then where was he phoning from?" Jack puzzled, putting down the tray of crockery on the table. "He was adamant he wasn't coming to mi granddad's funeral."

"Not coming?" his soon-to-be-mother-in-law answered. "That's not like William. Bit of a lazy person, but he always does the right thing eventually."

"I'll phone Val later on," Jenny said. "Now it's cup of tea time and—"

"Digestive?" Jack finished off, grinning, knowing what she was going to say next. He knew her so well.

"These," she interrupted him, smiling demurely, taking out a large flowered tin from the cupboard.

Jack's face explained the surprise and joy he felt. He loved nothing better than a surprise, especially when it promised food. He had half an inkling of what might be in the tin. Chocolate digestives perhaps? Or even…

"Home-made fruit scones!" he drooled. "How good does life get? Goes to prove my point that for every down side, there's an equally potent up side. Yes!"

"Where do you think your brother might have gone?" Jenny's mum asked through a mouthful of scone.

"No idea," Jack replied, equally muffled as he filled his mouth, not too concerned about anything but these wonderful scones. His brother was ten years older than him and could look after himself. It was no business of his what problems he and his wife were having. His only problem was persuading Jenny to pass him another scone.

Jenny's mother looked to her daughter for a better explanation, but got virtually the same response.

"If there's a problem," Jenny explained, "they'll either sort it out together, or—"

"Or?" her mother repeated emphatically.

"They'll part company and start again," Jenny went on.

"Jenny," her mum gasped. "How could you? She—"

"Ignored my problems when I was stuck on my own trying to bring Jessie up," Jenny interrupted, "until she decided to poke her nose in when my Jack came to my rescue. Now we are the ones to be happy, aren't we, Jack?"

"Too right, we are," he mumbled through another mouthful of scone. "If she wants help, she'll ask, or come up here in person. Neither of them has wanted much to do with the old town – or the old family, for that matter."

They sat quietly finishing their afternoon cuppa, that some would have called high tea. His granddad would have called it high tea 'onny ifn tha sits on an 'igh stool'.

-o-

"Jack," Jim Stephenson shouted from the side room to the staff area at break time. "Jack … telephone."

"This Jack?" he laughed as he took the receiver.

"There's only one Jack in this school, daft bugger," Bill Jones quipped as he passed, cup of tea in hand, on his way to yard duty. "Thank goodness. And soon there won't be even that."

"Aww. Poor Bill," Jack clucked. "Will tha miss me?"

"Like a dose of the shits I will," Bill guffawed as he clicked the outside door.

"Hello? Jack Ingles here. Who is it?" he announced. "Line's a bad 'un so you'll have to speak up … William? That you?"

A mumbled 'yes' surrounded by crackle and hiss barely registered.

"Where the hell are you, and what are you playing at?" Jack snapped. "Castleford? What the hell—? No, I won't meet you there. I won't leave Jenny on her own. Been on her own all day with Jessie, and her morning sickness … Yes, if you must. We'll expect you at about seven … and for goodness' sake, phone Val. God knows what she's done wrong to you, but it can't be that bad. See you at seven, and … don't be late."

"OK?" Jim asked as Jack sat down with his mug of tea. He hadn't even had the chance to sniff his two digestives let alone eat them, and there was only five minutes left to his break.

"Thanks, Brother," he muttered.

"What are you thanking me for?" Jim asked, grinning as he watched him trying to stuff a full biscuit into his mouth at one go. "Hungry, Jack?"

"It's my stupid brother causing a nuisance of himself at home, and now I won't be able to finish my biscuit and tea. Spoil the rest of my day, it will," he muttered with difficulty through a mouthful of chocolate biscuit.

They laughed as they made for the door before the bell rang to summon the ranks to their battle stations.

Fortunately for Jack, he had a couple of free lessons at the end of the day, allowing him to steal a march on the official finishing time. He would clear it with the head at lunchtime to allow him to leave early on family business. Tom Matthews was a good head, in that he believed in pay-back. He appreciated all the extra efforts his teachers put in, making life exciting for students, and so much easier for him as head.

By leaving just half an hour early, Jack could cut travel time by a further half hour, missing almost all the bottlenecks between Crown Point Road and Hunslet Road. The jaunt through Methley and Whitwood became relatively easy at this time, too.

Before then, Form 1A needed amusing, and the sixth form had to be licked into shape.

"Jenny!" he shouted as he eased himself through the front porch into the front room. "I'm back. Jenny?"

No Jenny? This wasn't at all usual.

She always leaped at him as soon as he had cleared the inner front door. He scratched his head as he checked all the other rooms.

"Jenny?" he called again as he opened the back door on to their very own nine feet of brick yard. "Jen ... Val? What are you doing here? I spoke to William on the school's phone only this morning."

"This morning?" she gasped. "Where is he? Is he all right?"

"We'll find out in a couple of hours or so," he said. "He's coming here at seven."

Val covered her face with her hands, and broke down into sobs of relief mixed with anguish, as her sister put her arms around her shoulders.

"What's going on, Val?" Jack asked pointedly, as they trouped back into the front room where Jack would have his customary tea and biscuits. "He sounded ... upset, and you don't seem much different. Problems between you two?"

"Jack?" Jenny said quietly, lifting her eyebrows, hoping to avert a full-scale inquest into her sister's marital difficulties.

"No," Val interrupted, "you have a right to know. I was quick to challenge you two about your private affairs."

"Can we have a cuppa first, please?" Jack asked quietly. "Not been a wonderful day all round, I think."

"I'll—" Jenny said, trying to shuffle off the settee.

"You stay where you are," he advised softly. "You've had an even worse one, I should imagine. I'll get it."

"But—" she tried to protest.

"No buts," he went on. "Don't worry. I'll bring us a surprise."

"Oh yes?" they both laughed.

"And what's that?" Jenny said with a grin. "Tea and a … rich tea biscuit?"

"Don't forget," she shouted, as he disappeared into the bowels of their tiny kitchenette, "there are still some scones in that cake tin under the pantry stone."

"Six o'clock," Jack said polishing off the last of the scones on his plate, "and you still haven't told us what you think might be the problem between you and our William. You see, the way I—"

"Not your call to make, lovely," Jenny said, smiling at what she knew he was going to say. "We're here to give them space to air what's what, you know. We can't prejudge or pre-empt. So, let's wait and see, eh?"

"William, don't forget," Jack reminded them both, "has no idea you're here, Val. So, mightn't it be as well for us to talk things through a bit so we can help when you do meet?"

"Pragmatic as ever, eh, Jack?" Val agreed ruefully. "He's right. Of course he's right."

Silence hung around them politely for a few minutes, as if waiting for orders to disperse. Val was the one to give that order.

"Hard to know where to start, really," she began. "William's become harder to connect with lately. More and more he's been … distant, and not wanting to spend time with me and the kids – or so it seems."

"He's never been good at expressing his feelings, for as long as I can recall," Jack said, drawing on his considerable stock of memories. "I remember—"

"Jack?" Jenny interrupted gently. "Val's story?"

"What? Oh, sorry," he smiled. "Just getting carried away a bit there. Sorry."

"To cut a long story short," Val went on quietly, "I became friendly with another young teacher at school, who had, in fact, been appointed at the same time as me. The weird thing was that we were in the same group at college."

"Young teacher, as in—?" Jack asked, more than a little puzzled that this should have caused problems.

"Alan," Val replied, "had always fancied me throughout, but he understood about William, and all that. Anyway, we became more friendly as time went on, and—"

"You didn't…?" Jenny asked, aware of Jack's unease and disquiet next to her on the settee. "I mean—?"

"No," she said hesitantly, "we didn't, but it would have been so easy. Alan's a gentleman, you see, and would never take advantage, even though he knows how things are between William and me. Don't get me wrong. I love my husband, but sometimes – just sometimes – it seems that he doesn't feel the same about me."

"If this has been between just you and this Alan," Jenny puzzled, "you know, a simple friendship, how does William have to be involved? I mean, Jack knows I have female and male friends that he doesn't know – or care about, for that matter – but he would never cause a fuss or become jealous."

"He didn't know," Val went on, "that is until someone whom we both know, I assume, told him I was having an affair."

"No," they chorused, not believing that some interfering busybody should poke their well-meaning – or mischievous – nose in.

"What did you do?" Jenny asked, alarmed at what she

might be about to say.

The question remained in the air, floating like a bad smell that no-one wants to acknowledge, when it's answer was interrupted by a tentative tapping at the front door. Val's look of horror at realising that her husband had arrived betrayed her feelings.

"Come in, William," Jack shouted. "It's open."

Val watched William's shadowy form through the frosted glass walls of the tiny front vestibule with trepidation. She guessed what his reaction might be when he saw her unexpected frame sitting in the front room, but she was staying there anyway.

"Val?" he said, a surprised gasp escaping his lips as he turned into the room. "What are you doing here? I'll just—"

Expecting this sort of ponderous response from his brother, Jack leaped to his feet in an instant, and, knocking over the tray, he snecked the inner door, and directed William to another chair before he could escape.

"Before you jump to one of your ridiculous conclusions as to why we are all sitting here waiting for the next spectre to attend the feast," Jack said quickly, "Val dropped in unexpectedly. We didn't plan this. OK?"

"But why is she here?" William replied, turning towards him.

"Does she take sugar?" Jenny asked sarcastically, her figuratively rhetorical question skimming the top of his head.

"What do you mean?" William asked, a deeply puzzled frown invading his face.

"That she is sitting there, and you should ask her," Jack explained, a patronising smile lighting his face.

"Don't patronise me, Jack," William snarled.

"Or what?" he answered. "Don't be such a bloody fool, William. You need to talk to your wife, who has done nothing wrong."

"Is that her talking," William snapped, "or do you have some divine spirit moving your lips? My reliable source tells me she's having an affair, so would you like to explain why I should believe you or her?"

"Because she is your wife," Jenny butted in. "Isn't that enough? How long have you been married? How many children have you made together? How much of a support has she been to you in your professional life? How much of a saint has she been to put up with your stupidly boorish ways of late?"

"Shades of our childhood, eh, William?" Jack said quietly. "I remember, even if you don't."

William slumped back in his chair, an air of resignation about him.

"So where have you been these last few days?" Val asked him quietly. "The children have missed you desperately. I've missed you, too. Hasn't your school missed you?"

"Been on a three-day PE course at Carnegie College in Headingley, Leeds," he replied, puzzled why she might be asking. "I told you I'd applied several weeks ago."

"But you didn't speak to me about it before you went," she explained quietly, not wanting to start another stand-off.

"I'm sure I did," he answered with a shrug. "Anyway, it was residential so my school knew about it and made arrangements for cover."

Val let the reasoning behind that answer go by, which she had had to do a lot recently. It seemed that her husband was unwilling to take responsibility for his own actions lately.

"Can I assume you two would like to talk?" Jack's gravelly voice shredded the silence. "If so, we'll take Jessie for a walk to the park and feed the—"

"I'd rather you stayed, Jack," Val interrupted quickly, "if you don't mind."

"Me?" he replied. "Not at all."

"Then I'll stay as well," Jenny decided. "Time for Jessie's nap, anyway."

William shuffled uncomfortably in his chair, feeling claustrophobic and trapped by this human fence. He glowered at his wife for forcing him into this predicament, and couldn't wait until it was over.

"Well, William?" Jack said, leaving him in no doubt as to where his loyalties lay. "We're on the edge, I feel. What's it to be?"

-o-

Jud Holmes' funeral was the second most hurtful and depressing event of Jack's life, signifying the final resting of the most influential man in his time on this earth. Marion couldn't bear to have his body at home for folks to gawp at, so he had to remain at the hospital's chapel of rest until he was prepared for burial and brought to his home by the undertaker, to start his last journey.

Ever the romantic, Jud had said, he had already bought and paid for a plot for two in Normanton's cemetery next to the one occupied by daughter Flo. "A family corner," he called it, which would grow, hopefully, to accommodate the whole clan.

Never one to show her feelings, Marion walked steadfastly and purposefully, mouth set in an emotionless tight-lipped line, directly behind the pall-bearers from her front door. The black hearse stood, tail gate gaping, ready to welcome its passenger for his last earthly journey. A light drizzle coated everything it touched as the coffin slid noiselessly into its glass tomb in preparation for its consignment to its final resting place.

True to form, William arrived an hour before the interment and left before the reception, barely allowing him time to pay decent respects to the passing of a giant of a man whose influence on their lives had been incalculable.

"Is tha not stopping for tea, lad?" Marion asked him as he prepared to take his leave outside the Majestic Café. "Thi Granddad would have wanted thee to be there."

"Long journey back, Grandma," he apologised, "and I wasn't able to get time off work."

Jack knew that that wasn't true, but he held his counsel for another time. No doubt William had his reasons, but this was neither the place nor the time to challenge them in public. They shook hands, said little, and parted on a terse and tense note, the one promising to phone the other in due course. Jack knew that would never happen any time soon, unless his hand was forced by his wife or children.

Jack put his arm around Grandma's shoulders, and in her one and only public show of capitulation to rising emotion, she lay her head against his shoulder, and shed quiet tears as a final farewell to her beloved Jud.

"Until the next time, you big lummox," she whispered. "Until the next time."

Chapter 13

"Thin end of the wedge, if you ask me," Jack said categorically, early Sunday morning as he was helping Jenny out of her warm pit. Things were becoming more uncomfortable for her, as her mountainous baby bump made any sort of mobility nigh on impossible without help.

"What is?" she asked once she was upright.

"Problems wi' your Val and our William," he replied.

"In what way?" she insisted. "Because, if you mean with their marriage, then I don't agree. Do you mean that?"

"Yes, I do," he went on.

"But that was sorted out weeks ago," she said, concerned though not really surprised he had brought it up again. You had to expect that with Jack. Throughout his life, questions could simmer for months, only to resurface when you were least expecting them.

"Only saying," he added with a shrug of his non-committal non-judgemental shoulders. "If it's surfaced once, what does that say about the state of their marriage? How could he even think that about Val? She's not as good as her sister, but she's better than most."

"You say the loveliest things, my beautiful man – sometimes," she replied with a laugh as she draped herself about his neck, wincing slightly as her bump made brief contact with his body.

"Sex out of the question, then?" he laughed, as he took

hold of her elbow to help her to the bathroom. "Come on then, owd love, I'll help you in."

They both laughed as he helped her across the landing as if she were a hundred and three.

The strident, ear drum shattering fire bell of a telephone drowned their conversation, startling them to the edge of panic. Nobody should be allowed to make that sort of telephone call at this time on a Sunday morning.

"Can you manage on your own, Jen," Jack asked, "or do you need me to give you a swill and brush?"

"Get on with you, lummox," she laughed. "Answer the phone."

Lummox? By 'eck! That took him back, and brought tears to his eyes, it did. Jud Holmes, thou big lummox! If only Marion was able to call him that now, and he could respond in like fashion.

"Hello? And who's calling at this ungodly hour of a Sunday morning?" Jack said as he lifted the receiver. Jenny smiled as she sat on the edge of the bath, wiping and moisturising her face. That was her lovely man. How lucky she was to have him at last, and to be carrying his child, although at times it seemed as if it was carrying her.

"Jenny," Jack called from the bottom of the stairs. "Not back in bed are you?"

"Cheeky bugger," she laughed, craning her neck round the bathroom door. "Who was that?"

"Twenty past nine, my beautiful lady," he replied. "Time to get a move on. We've got visitors mid-afternoon."

"Oh no," she sighed. "Not Val and William and their tribe again. I knew we shouldn't have left them with an open invitation."

"Three people we already know?" he prodded.

"Three?" Jenny puzzled. "Ah ... Irene, David and Jessie?"

"The very same," he laughed. "Is that all right? Only ... they seemed to want to come. For what reason, we will find out this afternoon."

"I think the first thing we'll do with our new house," Jenny said, shivering slightly with the cold as she moved around the front room, "will be to have central heating and this new-fangled secondary glazing put in."

The fire grate threw out a goodly amount of heat, but it consumed the coal they used hungrily, greedily – warming you only if you sat in direct line. There were many areas in the room that harboured lurking icy monsters ready to leap on the unsuspecting. In the room where the fire couldn't reach, bodies had to be clad according to strict sub-arctic conditions. Oh, for the heartening warmth of central heating to unify all their living spaces.

By early afternoon, too, the icy frost fingers scrabbling desperately to keep hold of the window panes, were beginning to melt, and feeling the fire's boot up their collective backsides.

"Jack, quick!" Jenny shouted urgently. He shot into the front room as if the hounds of hell were snapping at his shirt tails, to see her with her hands holding her belly. "Quick, put your hands here. Feel it?"

"Wow," he gasped, as a hefty kick ricocheted up his arm. "That's ma boy."

He slipped his arm around this beautiful lady and kissed her tenderly, slowly, pouring every ounce of love into her, as his chest swelled with pride at what they had finally achieved. At last, after all the trials they shouldn't have had to experience, they were now where they should have been five years before. Although those lost years had been painful in many ways for them both, they looked on them as 'training' for what was to come.

The difficulty now was not to rush ahead to try to make up for lost time, but Jack wasn't about to let that happen, no matter what the free-thinking Jenny might want. His pragmatism had always guided him up to press, and he wasn't about to allow it to desert him – them – now.

"Do you know what I like about you, Jack Ingles?" Jenny said, looking up at his face as she was snuggled close to him on the settee.

"My dashing good looks? My unbelievably razor-sharp wit?" he smiled, lids half-closed, enjoying the calm, easy closeness to his soul mate.

"The way you have everything sorted out in your head," she said, ignoring his self-deprecating hyperbole, as she always did. "Your lovely mind has it all sorted out as to what comes next, when we can afford it, and when it can be done. It's all in there, and all so sensibly ordered. All this for us as a family, and that's why I love you. You are such a thoughtful and patient man that I can't wait for the rest of my life to roll. Rock on, Our Jack."

A discreet rattle of the front door letterbox eased them out of their collective reverie, and ushered Jack to let their friends in.

"'Ello Jack," a gutturally unpleasant voice, laced with a vague overtone of stale Tetley's, washed over his face. "Is tha goin to let me in?"

"Father," Jack spat back, flattening the sound of the name to its insulting extreme. "What does thy want? Come to try to weedle thi way in, to spoil my life now, like tha did wi' mi mam?"

"Na, just thee 'odd on a bit," Eric said, trying to inject as much of a warning into his words as he could.

"No, thee 'odd on," Jack snarled, cutting through his father's venom. "Thy threats hold no fear for me anymore, old man. Tha can't intimidate me like thy used to when I was a nipper. If thy hadn't but noticed, I'm a lot older, and a lot bigger now. So, what does tha want?"

"Isn't tha goin' to ask me in?" Eric repeated, swapping his aggressive body language for a more placatory one. "Tha sees, I've heard as tha's expecting, and I've browt thee sum money to 'elp young 'un into t'world a bit more easy like."

"No. Tha's not crossing my threshold," Jack said, thrusting his face aggressively towards his father. "Not now, not ever. So tha can shove thi money up thy arse, and tha can bugger off."

"Or else?" Eric said, bravado rising. However, he neither understood what his son had become, nor expected his reaction, as Jack pulled himself to his full height and size. That was enough to make Eric back off in shocked surprise.

"Perhaps if tha'd treated mi mam better, and not kept her short o' brass," Jack growled, "t'reception might have been a mite different. Now tha's had thi say, don't come back, because next time I might not be so generous."

"Who was that, my lovely?" Jenny asked as she brought cakes and other goodies into the front room, ready for their friends, although she had heard almost every word.

"Just an old nobody I used to know," he answered, "of no consequence ... Wow. Look at all this. You are the most generous and thoughtful person on this earth, and I should be extremely surprised if David wasn't able to smell that from Leeds."

A firm and business-like rattle at the door told him ...

"That's David," Jack laughed. "Never one to turn up a chance to feed his face. David ... Irene ... Irene?"

"Well, this is a surprise and no mistake," he went on, once he had ushered them through the front door.

"Now it's our turn to say 'snap'," David guffawed as they disrobed. "Both expecting at roughly the same time, me thinks."

"Due March third," Jenny laughed, not losing sight of its significance.

"Me too," Irene echoed. "How spooky is that?"

"So, this is really worth celebrating," Jack said, happy to hug his cousin, bearing in mind her bump was just as difficult to negotiate as Jenny's. "Do you realise the significance of your combined due dates, Irene?"

"Auntie Flo's…?" she replied quietly, recognising the saddening look growing in his face. "She will be involved at last, and I'm sure she will know."

"Did I see Uncle—?" Irene continued.

"Someone of no consequence or importance to either of us, really, Irene," Jack interrupted, "who won't be bothering us again."

She, of all people, understood, for the warring years between her mother and two other uncles – and Jack's father – had been a jarring part of her own growing up. It had been a significant catalyst, too, in determining the path she had taken. Fortunately, however, the upside had seen the introduction of two very important men to her life, and for that she would be eternally grateful.

"We thought we might be able to bring a bit of surprise and sunshine into your otherwise dull and mundane lives, dear boy," David joked, a smile growing at his mouth corners, "but we can never upstage you, can we?"

Jenny laughed at David's off-beat sense of humour, and said, "You know my Jack by now, surely, David? He'll always surprise you."

"I have another piece of good fortune to share with you," David said, once tea and coffee were made and poured, and as Jenny's baking was slid under David's sensitive nose. "Well, for me at least."

"Don't tell me they've gone and made you head teacher," Jack hazarded a stab, with a shrug and a cheeky grin.

"Funny you should mention that," David replied, an even cheekier grin on his face.

"No! Never!" Jack whooped. "Really? But what about the Barchester Chronicles?"

"He's gone down with a severe bout of the lurgies and will be off for another couple of months," David said, trying not to show his delight too much. "So … they've said that without me in the hot seat, they would have to shut the school."

"Yea! Right!" Jack guffawed, pulling out his tongue in derision. "Head Honcho Aston, eh? Brilliant."

"My problem now is that I don't have anyone who could be my deputy," David said in quiet earnest.

"And that is what to do with me?" Jack replied, a seriously puzzled look betraying his lack of understanding.

"Well, I was wondering if there might be any chance of your taking over," he replied, "sort of for the time being."

"Nothing I'd like better, old chap," Jack answered, to a huge smile from David. "Only two minor things standing in my way, really. For one, I am pretty sure Tom Matthews, my head, may not be as enthusiastic – and two, I have a new job myself for September. So, I think I may have to duck out on this one."

"A new job?" Irene asked. "You're a dark horse keeping that one close to your chest. Since when?"

"Oh, a few weeks ago," he replied. "Not told you because we've not seen you for a while."

"Onwards and upwards, eh, old chap?" David said. "Shame you aren't still at Broughton."

"Still," Jack replied, an almost imperceptible shrug supporting what he had to say, "as head of year, it gives me a start on the ladder, which is perhaps my best area – and the money's good. Don't forget I have a high-maintenance wife and two children to support."

"Wife?" Jenny queried, somewhat surprised by his words. It wasn't like Jack to make such an important mistake.

"Didn't I tell you?" he said, a wicked smile decorating his cheeky face. "I got a call from our solicitor to say that my decree nisi is through, oh … and yours."

"You—" Jenny laughed, whizzing a cushion at his head, which he headed onto the clear table, much to the two

Jessies' amusement.

"How about popping down to the registry office next Saturday, and getting hitched?" Jack suggested, seriously.

"Hang on a bit, Buster," Jenny cut in sharply. "I understand your urgency to make an honest woman of me, but this will be my day, and so you're going to have to defer to my wishes. Besides, March third isn't that far away, and I'd like to have both our children present – physically."

"OK. Just saying," he added, hands above his head in surrender. "You're the boss."

"I take it we'll be invited?" Irene asked.

"Course you will," Jenny agreed. "How could we leave out our bestest friends ... David as well, naturally?"

Jack cracked out laughing, as did the other two.

"Love it," he continued, chuckling in the background. "That's ma girl. In fact there's a distinct chance you two – and Jenny's mum – might be our only guests."

"What about your grandma and your brother?" Irene asked, a quizzical look heralding her confusion. "Won't he and his family be invited?"

"Invited, yes," Jenny explained, "but it's by no means certain they'll come, even if we tell them how important it is that they should be part of it."

Irene wasn't too sure what to make of this. She understood how dysfunctional and fragmented Jack's arm of her family was, but she had never heard of such disharmony – not at a time like this, anyway.

"Long story," Jack explained with a sigh and a resigned shrug, "but problems in their camp I won't bore you with. Life's never dull or straightforward in this family, eh, cousin? Grandma won't be a problem. She's included automatically in whatever we decide to do."

Since Irene had come to know this young man, she had never known anything, any happening, to faze him or to derail his calculated pathway. She knew he was a disciple of two almost opposite philosophies on life: – on the one hand, organised, pragmatic, ordered; on the other, whatever was going to happen would, and nothing would divert that. He lived his life according to those principles with one proviso: – if an unplanned opportunity presented itself to him, he would grab it with both hands and embrace where it might take him.

He was a complex individual to many people, but reasonably straightforward to those who knew him well. The two things you could always guarantee with Jack were honesty and plain speaking – traits not palatable to many, but crucial elements that would help in understanding him and his ways.

"And I thought my life was complicated sometimes," David said, a wry smile betraying his awe at how his friend handled his life. "So, will your wedding go ahead, what with not knowing which way your brother will vote?"

"What he might do or not do is irrelevant to us," Jack explained slowly. "It would be better if they came – and I truly believe Val and the kids will – but if they don't, it won't either divert or spoil what we plan. Jenny is going to have what she's always wanted and never been able to have – until now. I've got what I want now, but it has to be made official, even though it's a year or two late."

With a look of deep love and respect in her eyes, she waddled over to this man, slid her arm around his waist, and kissed him gently on the cheek. She was happier now than she ever thought she would be, and the hurt and uncertainty from all those years was wiped away, because this man had walked purposefully back into her life, where he wanted to be and where he belonged.

Chapter 14

"Mr Matthews?" Jack's voice echoed into the black hole that was their phone line. "Sorry, but I won't be in today. Jenny's waters broke and shortly we'll be on our way to the hospital."

"Jack," Tom Matthews reassured him, "Friday's an easy day and I have it covered. Just do what you have to do, take as long as you need, and I'll make sure every thing's taken care of at this end from Monday. And ... good luck with the birth, though in truth you're not the one I should be saying that to."

Jack laughed at his crackly end of the line, thanked his head, and hung up.

"Ready for off, my beauty?" he smiled, reassuring Jenny that he wouldn't leave her, and would be there to welcome his new baby with her.

"No," she replied, squeezing his hand, as they headed for the door, "but let's go anyway. It feels like she could be joining us at any time."

Friday second of March ... almost six years to the date since his mam's passing, and now a new baby about to make its entry to this beautiful world. Sadness tinged his joy, but his mam wouldn't have allowed self-pity. She would have wanted to be there; to be part of it all; to be cheering them on.

"She?" Jack asked, but not questioning female intuition.

Jenny had been in tune as long as he had known her. What did she say she was? Psychic? That day had stayed with him, though he remembered it overlaid with a healthy slice of scepticism. Their time together had since taught him otherwise.

"Yeah," she said, breathing heavily to try to control the inevitable. "Just a feeling. The other feeling is that if we don't get a move on, we'll be taking her to the hospital with us. Car please, Jack. Now!"

Although she had hoped otherwise, Jenny's labour was long, arduous, and exhausting. At two minutes to four in the morning on March third, Florence May Ingles made her leisurely entry to this brave new world; a world that was now ready to see and welcome her. Little Flo had entered the building quietly, like the little lady she was.

The only resemblance she bore to her father was a pair of deep green pools that looked steadfastly into this generally hasty world, as if to say, "Look! I'm here. Let's take things slowly, if you please. What's the hurry?"

Her hair was certainly nothing to do with Jack. Unusually long, dark, and with a definite turn, although it was difficult to tell at this stage, it came either from Jenny's mother or Jack's mam. Apart from a weak whimper on entry after her first gulp of air, she made little noise to remind them she had arrived. She didn't need to. All eyes were definitely on her serenely smiling face.

"She has green eyes," Jack noticed, a flush of warm, loving pride suffusing his beaming face. "Jenny, she's beautiful. Thank you."

He slid his arms around her and kissed her in gratitude.

"Tired," she muttered. "Need to sleep."

"OK, Mr Ingles," the nurse in charge said quietly, "time for you to go. Mrs Ingles needs as much rest as possible after such a long labour, and I suspect that, at quarter past four in the morning, so do you. Come back in another twelve hours to see your lovely family cleansed and rested."

He kissed Jenny's already closed eyelids, and, loath to leave, crossed the delivery room threshold, ready to dish out those metaphorical cigars to the world.

"I think you'll find the eye colour will change," the nurse said. But Jack knew differently. Florence May was his daughter, and what she had now would stay with her. Of that he was convinced.

The world was a different place at this time of day. Quiet and calm, with a distinct chill and the threat of rain in the air, it allowed Jack to luxuriate in what he had just witnessed. He felt nothing but awe and love for this woman who had just given him the beautiful daughter he could cherish and spoil.

"Well, Jack, lad," he muttered, as the Mini spat into life, "your own daughter at last. Welcome to the space your grandma left for you. If you turn out to be half as good as her, Florence May, you'll do for me."

The tranquil countryside between Wakefield and Normanton sped by almost unnoticed as his thoughts and feelings were consumed by recent events. The Mini growled and complained as it protested the trials of Pineapple Hill on its way up to and past Sharlston Common and the new road, before the descent to the Terrace and Dodsworth Junior School. This motor, though a good economical friend, would have to be replaced by something more appropriate for carrying a growing family – a shooting brake, perhaps?

Their little house was quiet and still. Although warm enough at this time of year in very early spring, it wouldn't do any more for their unpredictably colder months. He wouldn't countenance another winter here, especially with a toddler and a new baby to look after.

A cup of steaming tea in hand, he stood by the front window gazing across Queen Street at … more houses starring back at him. He longed for openness and the space he felt he needed but had never had. The new house up Warmfield way, on the edge of town, overlooking Goosehill fields – which he had played in and explored as a nipper – would do them just fine. Big enough for his expanding brood, it gave him enough scope to develop further.

He flopped onto the settee, thoughts of the date flooding into his mind. It wasn't so different from this time six years before, that his mam had left him, and he had felt so bereft, so lost, so alone. Tears rushed to his eyes and trickled down his cheeks in unashamed, unabated sorrow that she of all people wasn't here to witness the joy he would have loved to share with her. His eyes closed slowly, as he drifted away.

Saturday third of March crept by until early morning turned into early afternoon. Jack awoke with a start, a badly aching neck, a numb left arm, and a mouth like a tram driver's glove.

"My God. What the—?" he uttered as the light of twelve noon hit his disorientated eyes. He pushed himself out of the settee with a groan and a grimace of discomfort, wondering why he wasn't now sliding out of a warm bed next to an equally warm Jenny. His brain finally clanged into this real world of fatherhood and joy.

"I'm a father ..." he grinned, "again."

His mind shot back to Jenny's struggle with pain and exhaustion. He had been there. He had seen it all. He had shared in her anguish. He had felt her concerns, her joy, and her unbelievable tiredness.

"Time?" he muttered, still not quite in the real world. "What's the bloody time?"

Quarter past noon. When was it the nurse had said to go back? Twelve hours was it? That would be...

"Bugger," he growled. "That's onny three and three quarter hours away. Got to get ... a move on."

Shave, wash, change of clothes, make himself

half-decent, and then there was the surprise he had been planning what seemed like ... forever. She'd like that. Meck things ... official, like. Aye. His owd granddad woulda thowt that were a rayt grand idea. He'd already run it past his grandma, and she had smiled in appreciation.

"Tha's an old romantical, Our Jack," she had said finally, trying to reach his spikes to stroke his head. He had stood on his tip toes so she wasn't able to reach, to make her laugh and take her out of herself. Jud's death was still very raw, and probably would be for the rest of her life.

He hadn't felt so much tiredness and so much lethargy for a long time. 'E would 'after sheck 'issen out of it if he were to reach t'ospital in time to see 'is lasses rayt off.

"Plenty o' time," he muttered. "Porridge first and then. No use wi' out mi porridge."

His mam would have reminded him about that first time at breakfast in Mrs Ridge's guest house in Blackpool. Now, that was a holiday worth remembering ... memorable on many accounts.

His mind drifted back to that time he spent with his granddad; how he felt a pang of guilt because he had left him asleep, unprotected, in his deck chair on the front. He could see the scene, smell the mixture of fish and chips, vinegar-soaked cockles, and wafts of the sea, plain as day. The swazzle-induced cackle of Mr Punch assaulted his eardrums, along with the rattle of the wooden crocodile's jaws trying furtively to chomp on the flailing string of sausages as it whizzed past Punch's head.

-o-

Car parking at the hospital was difficult but not impossible for Jack. He could squeeze his little Mini into many a space larger cars wouldn't even contemplate.

Tapping his pocket as he strode along the by now bustling glass tunnel to check his 'surprise' for Jenny was still there, he smiled in that self-satisfied way that told the world everything was in order, just as he had planned it.

Quarter past four on the dot, he strode purposefully through the door into the ward to see her, his Jenny, sitting up in bed craning her neck to check on his arrival. Once she had seen those spikes pointing the way, a huge grin split her face, mirroring his, and her shuffling gingerly back in the bed told him she was dying to feel his arms around her.

He buried his face in her hair and kissed her tenderly, as he held her body tightly next to his.

"Steady, tiger," she urged quietly. "A bit sore."

He sprang back, a look of horror on his face that he might have hurt her in any way.

"Not that sore," she laughed. "Well, what do you think of her?"

He turned slowly to see a tiny bundle of clothing nestling in a transparent crib the other side of Jenny's newly-changed, white-covered bed.

"That's our..." he gasped quietly, a look of delight mingled with awe and surprise. Her clear green eyes were open, and she seemed to be gazing at this goliath, with a degree of puzzlement, as if trying to work out where he had come from. Suddenly, unexpectedly, she pulled her arms from under her covers and raised them slowly, unsteadily, towards Jack, as if daring him to pick her up.

"She wants you, Jack," Jenny assured him quietly, recognising that very rare look of indecision in his eyes. "You can pick her up, you know. She won't break. She is yours."

Unsure, he scooped her carefully into his arms, not daring to turn around or move while he had her.

"Breathe, Jack," she said with a smile. "Breathe, and come sit here by me."

He turned slowly, not taking his eyes from this precious, unblinking bundle, and sat down as bidden in the chair next to Jenny's bed, exhaling slowly as he did so.

"That wasn't too bad, was it?" Jenny laughed. "You'll get used to it … eventually … I hope."

"She's absolutely gorgeous," he whispered, looking over at Jenny.

"I've been thinking," she said quietly, "you do of course realise the significance of the date and time of our daughter's birth, so I want her to be called Florence May, after your mam."

"I should like nothing better," Jack stammered, not knowing what to say, as tears filled his eyes, "but what about what you want? I mean, we should at least talk about it."

"That is what I want," she explained simply, "and as you want it as well, there's nothing more to say. You need to register Florence May Ingles' arrival in this world as soon as possible."

"Thank you," he said in a hoarse whisper. "It means a lot."

He put his daughter back into her crib, and turned to Jenny as he sat down again. Digging into his jacket pocket, he fished out a small maroon box, and, gazing steadfastly into her eyes, he opened it slowly.

"I've been wanting to do this for some time, to make things official, like," he said quietly, a serious look on his face. "You know, proper."

With a final click of its lid, he turned the open box towards her, and whispered,

"Jenny, will you marry me?"

This was the last thing she had expected – a bunch of flowers or fruit, perhaps, yes, but not a huge diamond solitaire engagement ring.

"Oh, my God, Jack," she gasped when he slid it out of its box to slip it on to her finger. "It's gorgeous. How on earth did you—?"

He halted her words by laying his finger across her

lips, the slight inclination of his head and raised eyebrows reiterating his question.

"Of course I will, you daft bugger," she insisted, flinging her arms around his neck once the ring was safely on her finger. Gentle applause and mild cheers raced around the ward, recognising and sharing their joy.

"That's official, then," Jack said finally, his cheeks flushing vaguely with satisfaction.

"I love it," she insisted quietly, tears rolling down her cheeks. "You never cease to amaze me, Jack Ingles, and I can't wait to be your wife."

"Well," he went on, "as it happens—"

"You haven't," she gasped, a look of sheer surprise growing around her eyes.

"Actually," he grinned, "I ... haven't."

"You bugger," she burst out laughing, throwing a damp flannel at his head.

He put his arms around her and kissed her tenderly.

"Steady, tiger," she whispered in his ear.

"Sore?" he whispered back, stiffening.

"No," she giggled mischievously. "People watching."

"I'm watching you, too," a familiar voice crept up on them from behind Jack.

"Val?" Jenny said, not too sure why she was here. "I hope this is a good visit?"

"Can't I come and see my little sister," she smiled through a hug, "and my new niece?"

"Is everything—?" Jack ventured, after a slightly tentative hug.

"OK with William?" Val replied, an unconvincing smile hovering around her lips, and her eyes betraying her outward calm. "Yes, I think so. As far as I can tell."

Jenny shot a concerned glance at Jack, hoping he wouldn't pursue what was obvious to them both.

"Is he still at the secondary modern school?" Jack asked,

skirting the real issue, recognising and acknowledging Jenny's concern.

"He's quickly losing the feel for it, I'm afraid," Val said softly. "Talking about leaving teaching altogether … something about being disillusioned."

"That's disturbing," Jack frowned, "but I suppose I can understand where he's coming from."

"Anyway," Jenny butted in, recognising where this might be leading, "enough of that until another time, eh? What do you think of your new niece, Val?"

"She's gorgeous," Val cooed, as she cradled her unprotesting little body. "Thought of a name yet?"

"Florence May," Jenny replied, a smile of pride dancing about her mouth.

"Bit old-fashioned, don't you think?" Val said, a slight frown about her eyebrows. "Any reason…?"

"Mi mam's names," Jack said, his unblinking eyes looking into hers. "Jenny's suggestion. She was born almost exactly six years – to the day and time – since mi mam died. So, we thought—"

"It was a sign," Jenny added, to Val's embarrassment and discomfort. "So, Florence May Ingles it is."

"You see," Jack added finally, "Jenny and I don't let fashion dictate our life. We will live it as we see it, and anyone who doesn't agree with us doesn't matter anyway."

Chapter 15

"Morning, Jacky Boy," Bill said, slapping him on the back as they both entered school. "Congratulations in order?"

"Too right," Jack replied, a great grin glued to his face since he had brought home his two females from hospital. He had been loath to leave, but Jenny's mother had volunteered to stay with them until he returned. Tom Matthews had allowed him five days to see to all he needed, and during that time he had registered his daughter – his daughter, eh? Sounded grand – and had booked the registry office for their wedding in April.

He had thought it might make a rayt grand surprise to organise it himself without telling her, but a terminal bout of cold feet made him rethink. She was the one to suggest April seventh. And now, it was Wednesday seventh of March and his brood was at home. However, what she didn't know was that they would be wed from their own home. He had finalised the purchase the day before, and had agreed a reasonable price and the date for signing. He had put in his request for a joint bank account with the Midland in the High Street, and all he needed now was Jenny's signature to make it legal.

Unfortunately, two things had wrenched his mind away from his job – the one was obvious, and the other would happen in five months or so.

Although he was looking forward to opening a new chapter at Merton Grange, a slight frisson of doubt began to bubble in his innards, very much like his change from Woodhouse Junior to t'Grammar School, and from there to teacher training college. He set himself very high standards of expectation, and a failure to achieve them would cause him intense self-doubt. He couldn't allow himself to fail.

"Bill?" he asked the older man as they shouldered their way into the staff room.

"Yes, my boy?" he answered. "What can I do you for?"

"Advice, really," Jack said, scratching his thatch, which he did whenever he had an insoluble problem. "We'll be moving into our first house soon, and I was wondering about improvements."

"My advice to you would be to live in it for at least twelve months," Bill advised, "and then see how things have gone and what needs changing to make things right. Better to hang on a bit, which will save you a lot of time, aggravation, and the inevitable bob or two. I'm sure your Jenny will appreciate the time you are taking 'to plan'."

"Thanks, Bill," Jack smiled. "Mi granddad always suggested it would be better to ask someone who was a lot older for advice."

"Cheeky bugger," Bill laughed. "Your granddad sounds like a wise man."

"Sounded," Jack corrected. "He's gone now."

"Sorry to hear that," Bill added. "Still, none of us'll last forever."

-o-

Jack's routinely mundane day passed slowly and without too much excitement. Watching the second hand take three times as long to sweep the face of his class clock wasn't to be recommended for anyone looking forward to the end of any day. This day was his last in school for this week, as he had been granted Thursday and Friday in his new school, which was empty of all but desks and chairs and educational paraphernalia.

He was expecting a busy couple of days, but the approaching evening with his wife-to-be and his daughters would usher that out of his mind until morning.

The traipse back to Normanton was a particularly slow and tedious affair. A lorry had jack-knifed, overturned, and shed its load of pink toilet rolls on the bend just before Methley Bridge over the Calder, and the traffic queue was slow-moving. Jack smiled at the thought of being taken short conveniently around the bend towards Three Lane Ends. The hill over the railway bridge and on to Four Lane Ends by Whitwood College, for once, was a breeze. Downhill past The Rising Sun, and the rugby field on Whitwood Common, where he had played many a successful game, flew by.

It was so good to escape the tiny interior of the Mini, and to see Jenny waiting for him on the top door step.

He hugged her as if he hadn't seen her for weeks, kissed her and whispered in her ear that he loved her – as he did several times every day.

"Hello, love," she replied, a smile decorating her already happy face. "Kettle's on the boil, ready for your—"

"Tea and nibble," he finished with a grin.

"Somebody here to see you," she said, taking his coat and bag. "Somebody you've not seen for a while."

"Joyce," he said, as she greeted him with a hug. "Long time no see. How is it that all the women around me seem to have become pregnant, with bumps so big you can't get around them?"

They all laughed as he sat down with a sigh of relief and pleasure to be home.

"We've just had our first," he said, sipping the mug of tea Jenny had brought from the scullery, "as you are no doubt aware. When are you due to present the world with my next godchild? You promised, don't forget."

"Three weeks," she replied. "John and I—"

"John?" he puzzled. "I thought your intended was called Kevin?"

"Kicked him into touch ages ago," she said with a nonchalant shrug. "Wouldn't commit, you see, and besides, he couldn't keep his fingers out of yon shop's till. Couldn't have my children fathered by a thief. Met and married John Walker, just over a year ago, and now … this."

"But are you happy, our lass?" Jack asked, a slightly concerned frown etching his forehead. "Joyce Walker, eh?"

"Course I am, daft beggar," she laughed. "Would I be carrying our baby if I weren't?"

"John Walker did you say?" Jack asked, recognising the name vaguely. "Stick Walker, from down t'bottom of Garth Avenue?"

"Aye," she replied, "and what of it?"

"I knew him at Grammar School," Jack added. "He were in my class in t'third year. Left to go to QEGS, if I remember right?"

"That's the one," she agreed, eyebrows lifting in surprise, "and yes, he did. Goodness' sake! That memory of yours, Jack Ingles. Our very own Leslie Welch the Memory Man."

"Ha ha … that's funny," Jack guffawed. "Did you ever get that house down Ash Gap Lane, or High Green Road in Altofts? I seem to remember that's where you wanted to be."

"We're having one built in Church Road in Altofts," she replied, a look of excitement chasing her smile. "Somewhere between High Green Road corner – you know, where Mrs Chadwick's shop used to be – and the library and cemetery on Church Road."

"Ooh … 'ark at you," Jack and Jenny chorused. "Posh."

"Well," Joyce smiled, "John's a teacher as well, and he's

just got a job at Martin Frobisher Junior School, which would be two or three hundred yards from our front door-to-be. Couldn't be better, really."

"Then I would say you've dropped on your feet, Joyce Walker," Jack said, giving her the biggest squeeze her bump would allow. "Can I assume, then, that you, like us, are living where you were the last time we met over coffee by the library?"

"Makes sense," she agreed. "Rent's negligible, and it's big enough – just. Probably be a bit cramped when the bump's sitting in its high chair. But still …"

"And how is the library managing without you?" he asked, expecting a funny answer from his long-time friend. "You know, falling about their ears?"

"Still there," she replied unexpectedly, "muddling along. I might even go back when yon is here. John doesn't want me to, but he says it's up to me. Don't know. We'll have to wait and see."

"You see, Jenny," Jack said, turning to his wife-to-be, "there are more sensible men in the world besides me. Oh, by the way, Joyce, we're traipsing down the aisle next month. If you're not in process of delivering, we'd love you to come. Give us chance to meet the lucky man you call husband."

"We'd love that, Our Jack," she replied, a huge grin betraying her joy. "Looks like you've got the right one this time, too."

-o-

Jack didn't have to be at Merton Grange until ten, so there wasn't too much pressure to rush-dash through the worst of each morning's traffic. It was at times like this, however, that he began to question the sense of traipsing so far to work every day. Jenny wasn't fussed; didn't have the affinity with the area that dictated she had to stay in Normy. So, it was his decision ultimately, and one she was happy to go along with. A brand-new four-bedroomed house in suburban Leeds had its attractions, but it didn't have the open fields close by that he used to luxuriate in as a nipper.

Had he chosen the house up Warmfield for the right reason, he wondered? Was it a dose of nostalgia-too-far that had jaundiced his choice? Warmfield was a long way away from shopping civilisation on foot for his Jenny, because he would need the car … whereas, the modern housing developments he had seen in North Leeds were a push bike ride away from his new school. Jenny could have the car and her freedom. Two young children? No-brainer. They hadn't signed the contract to buy yet, and so could back away at any time. These questions crowded his busy mind as he slid easily into Merton Grange's car park.

Built on three levels like a flat-topped greenhouse, this two hundred feet long twenty year old school boasted a sloping playground the size of a small football field. Excessive? Not so when you realised it had to be sufficient for close on nine hundred young bodies hurtling around at a million miles an hour most playtimes.

A further two hundred and ten nine year olds would have most of their lessons in six mobile classrooms, destined to be the realm of King Jack.

Caged tennis courts, a games field of three full-sized pitches, and a fibreglass-covered heated swimming pool made up the rest of the campus for the largest nine to thirteen middle school in the country.

Why was Jack excited to be here? What made it the best educational establishment he had been in?

One word – opportunity.

With a growing family, he had to seize every rising chance to advance his family's fortunes and comfort, allowing Jenny to follow her dreams, too, when they surfaced.

"Good morning, Jack," a gruff but authoritative voice

welcomed him as he stepped into a large open space between a rising set of concrete stairs to his left and yet another wall of glass to his right, which revealed a heavily curtained assembly hall of huge proportions. Greenhouse in aspect from without, it unfortunately carried none of the heat associated with such a structure within. Jack drew his jacket closer about his shoulders.

"Good morning, Bob," he responded to his new head teacher.

"Mr Byrne, if you don't mind," the head corrected quite firmly.

"Then, it ought to be Mr Ingles, too, surely?" Jack smiled, sure of himself, and true to his own sense of fair play.

The head glowered at him over his glasses, not sure what he was hearing or what to do with this youngster other than to ignore his very sharp answer. Jack showed due respect to his head's age and experience, but fair was fair. He wasn't a god, for goodness' sake. Probably had there been anyone else present to witness his pertness, Mr Byrne might have slapped him down harder. Wily old campaigner that he was, he would bide his time and see how this youngster might progress. If he didn't perform to his expectations, he might take further issue and put the whippersnapper in his place. Yet, he might find Jack a very different animal from the ones he had been used to keeping under his shiny heel.

Jack wasn't impressed at all both with his new place of work and with the man who was due to direct its development. His first impressions were almost always right, and this didn't bode well for his future there. Still, education was all about the children – wasn't it?

"Meeting in my room with all the other senior staff in twenty minutes, if you please," the head threw over his shoulder as he made for his office. The cracked, mock marble floor of this anti-crush hall he found himself in clicked and clacked to his heavy tread as he reached his sanctuary door.

Cold, humourless, unwelcoming, and sterile, both school and head teacher had begun to sow seeds of doubt in Jack's head. Why was he here? Perhaps things might improve? Yet, his first ten minutes had gone no way to persuade him that this might be nothing but a battle-ground where blood might be spilled.

The head's office was in stark contrast to the rest of the school. Quality new furniture added to its physical warmth to make the large room comfortable and welcoming. Half the size of a normal classroom, it bore already the trappings of opulence that none of the other rooms in the school would ever match, from expensive light fittings to thick pile carpet to solid oak desk.

By the time Jack had returned from his exploration of the mobile classrooms, the senior gathering had collected in Byrne's Bothy, waiting for his input to their meeting.

Tom, the deputy, and Connie, the senior mistress, he had met already, and delightfully friendly people they were, too. He knew nothing as yet about the other three heads of year, but they seemed affable enough.

Brian was a large man with a significantly ginger beard and incredibly mobile, laughing eyes, and while Patrick smiled little, he had an easy air about him. Jack was, however, a little uneasy about their fourth member. There was disturbingly more behind that disingenuous façade than his bottle bottom glasses would allow to escape. Munro was one of those dour Scots who faded into the background in any gathering that might threaten exposure, having learned from an early age that it wasn't necessarily a good thing to play your cards openly.

He had made his way reasonably successfully in a cut-throat educational world on the stepping stones of other, more able colleagues who had suffered setbacks under his

Glaswegian heel. Not a man to trifle with, Jack and he were destined to cross invisible swords on occasion, that Jack considered normal interaction, but could turn out to be a dirk between the shoulder blades from him.

The meeting itself served as an introduction, but solved and resolved nothing, which, to his cost, Jack was to discover was a blueprint for successive siblings. Consequently, the day proved to be a half rather than a full one. This gave him chance to eat his corned beef sandwiches at leisure in his car at the bottom of North Park Avenue, with his trusty Thermos supplying him copious amounts of his favourite hot tea. She was a diamond, was that Jenny. After such a sumptuous meal, he whizzed around the two new housing developments he had flagged before heading for home.

"Jenny," Jack called as he snecked the outside door behind him. "Jenny. I'm home."

Hiding behind the inner porch door in the front room, she hurled herself at him, which didn't surprise him at all, as she was always full of fun – every day. She clasped his laughing body close to her and kissed him as if she hadn't seen him for an age.

"How old are you?" he laughed, delighted she was in his arms. "Twelve?"

"I have a proposition for you," he went on, as they sat on the settee with a cup of tea.

"Can you wait until after tea?" she said, a grin spreading across her face.

"Sex-mad you are, do you know?" he laughed. "Fortunately."

She snuggled back in the cushions, as close to him as she could, glad he was back home, and thanking God she had him at last.

"The proposition is to do with our new home," he continued slowly, "you know … Warmfield?"

"Looking forward to it a lot," she replied. "Somewhere

bigger than this, with some outside space for Jessie and Flo to play in. Getting excited. When do we sign?"

"Well," he went on, "that's just it. I've been thinking."

"Should I call Dr Twist?" she laughed, knowing it would recall his grandma and granddad's repartee of several years before."

"Seriously though," he added, "are you really set on that one? Only, I had a look at a couple of developments not far from the new school. They have brand spanking new four-bedroomed detached houses with all mod cons for little more than yon up Warmfield. Central heating, too. We could—"

"I'll have one," she blurted out. "Gardens?"

"Two big ones," he assured her, surprised at her speed of response. "Back and front."

"Remember when we talked about moving before?" she said. "When I said I quite fancied Leeds? Well, I went along with your wish to live near Warmfield, and wasn't really fussed because anywhere with us all together was OK by me."

"Jenny," Jack whistled softly, drawing in air quietly through his teeth. "Then, it's a good job I haven't signed the contract. This coming Saturday, I should like to take you to Leeds to have a look at the houses on offer. Then you need to be honest with me about what you prefer. Deal?"

"I know already," Jenny said, rubbing her hands in excited anticipation.

"You can't do," he gasped. "You haven't seen them yet. How could you know?"

"I have had this image in my mind of the sort of house I should like for a very long time," Jenny went on, eyes glazing. "If any of the ones on offer come reasonably close, I'll know straight away. So, tomorrow you'd better give back word on yon house at Warmfield, hadn't you?"

Chapter 16

"Mam!"
"Yes chick, what is it?"
"Mam?"
"Yes ch—"
Jack woke with a start.
Same recurring dream.
Same time every day. Ten minutes before the alarm.
Same result. A feeling of crushing sadness, swept away by unbridled elation, that he was alive with the woman of his dreams sleeping peacefully by his side.

As he turned over to kiss her, she drew him towards her, feeling him hard against her. Their love making was gentle, loving, and sensually satisfying as they reached climax together, in unison as always. They lay in each other's arms, enjoying that post-coital fuzzy warmth and comfortable togetherness they had come to value over the relatively short time they had been together.

"Bad dream, my sweet man?" Jenny asked, stroking his hair.

"Not really," Jack replied. "Same dream, same time, same place."

"Your mam?" she asked quietly.

"Aye," he sighed, a slight lump rising in his throat. He had no idea what it all meant; whether it had any significance at all, even. There must be something, or why would he have the same dream night after night?

"Same dream, every night?" she asked, not quite understanding how he could be sure. "How do you know?"

"Not quite the same," he said, a wry smile changing his features. "There is always one subtle change, I think, from the previous one. I can see it in detail soon after waking, but it disappears from my conscious mind soon after that. I suppose a modern-day Joseph might be able to tell me what I need to know, but I'm sure I have no idea."

He could hear stirrings from the children as he kissed Jenny and started to rouse himself. The electric fan heater downstairs began to whirr into his consciousness as it started to take the edge off the sitting room's chill.

"Anyway," he said as he sat up, "children to wash and feed, breakfast to cook, and our new house to choose. Time to be up."

He leaped out of bed and jerked the bedclothes with him, exposing her naked body to the cold. Leaping after him, she chased him into the bathroom wielding a pillow over her head like a limp claymore, ready to swipe his bouncing buttocks.

"You bugger," she laughed. "Now I'll have goose pimples in all the wrong places. Where are you?"

Once in the bathroom, he jumped out at her from behind the door, grabbed her to him and kissed her passionately. She dropped the pillow and relaxed into his arms.

"Jack," she whispered urgently. "Children? Breakfast?"

"Damn," he sighed. "I forgot. I was just getting ready to—"

"I know what you were getting ready to do," she interrupted him with a laugh. "No time now. Children? Jessie's getting restless, and I can hear Flo whimpering. I'll see to them, and you get breakfast."

"How do you fancy … porridge, for a change?" he smiled.

"Why did I know you were going to suggest that?" she laughed.

"Probably because I'm the best porridge maker in the world?" he said.

"Because you can't do anything else more like," she guffawed. "Now, down boy, and do your thing."

-o-

"That porridge was—" she started as an insistent rattling at the front door interrupted her.

"I'll get it," Jack said, already halfway up from their leisurely table.

"May I see Jenny, please?" a light male voice crept through to the front room.

"And who might you be?" Jack asked affably enough, though this smallish dark-haired man had just interrupted a pleasant family get-together. "Wait there and I'll see if she's available. Your name is—?"

"Barry," the man replied. "Tell her it's Barry. She'll know."

"A man called—" Jack started once he had regained the front room.

"I know," she replied, a stern look surprising him. "I heard."

"And?" he replied.

"He's Jessie's biological father," she replied sharply, "and I've no doubt he'll want to see her."

"Then he'll have to want on," Jack said, angry that that wastrel had had the temerity to call at his door. "I'll get shut of him."

"No, Jack," Jenny replied quite firmly, as she made for the door. "I'll speak to him. You stay here."

He tried to hear what was being said, but voices were muffled by the closed inner porch, until the door burst open. A man's body hurtled into the room, bounced off

Jack's solid frame, and crumpled at his feet. Jack picked this sorry pile from the floor by the scruff and manhandled him to the outside door.

"Now tell me," he threatened, "if you know of any reason why I shouldn't throw you into the road."

The man muttered something incoherent, finding it extremely difficult to speak with his shirt collar screwed tightly around his throat and over his mouth.

"I thowt not," Jack continued throwing him through the open door, "and if you come around here again, upsetting my family, I'll break your bloody neck. Understood?"

Jack made an exaggerated move, fists clenched, towards his prostrate body which was draped partly over the step but mainly on the pavement. Barry shot to his feet, a seriously alarmed look on his face, and legged it around the corner on to Church Lane, looking over his shoulder as he did so.

"Jack Ingles," Jenny gasped, a look of awe dominating her face. "You—"

"Anyone who threatens my family, Jenny," he said calmly, "has me to deal with, and I'm not big on bullying bravado either. If he comes back I'd be surprised, but I will carry out my threat if he does."

"Nobody's ever done that for me before," she said, snuggling her head next to his chest.

"You've never had me to fight your corner up to now," he said with a triumphant smile. "Cassius Marcellus Ingles, that's me. Float like a butterfly sting like a bee."

She laughed at his grotesquely dancing caricature of the boxer's shuffle, and sat down to another cup of tea.

"Mammy?" a little voice piped up from the stairs door.

"Yes, my lovely?" Jenny answered as she scooped her daughter into her arms. "What is it?"

"Is it time to get up yet?" Jessie said, a little frown of concern decorating her dark brows. "Only ... I want to wee again, and Fl ... Flow ... Flower ... my sister, smells ...

and..."

"I'm on my way, little one," Jenny laughed, looking over her shoulder at Jack, who was already heading towards the kitchen to get her breakfast, a huge guffaw erupting from his grinning face.

-o-

"And this is my favourite," Jack said, as he held open the show house front door. "Detached, four bedrooms, central heating, reasonably sized front and back gardens …"

Jenny simply stood in the lounge, her mouth open in surprise, and a tear glistening in her eye corner.

"That's not fair, Jack," she whispered hoarsely. "This is so big and … lovely … and we can't possibly afford it."

"Got something else to show you," he replied, suppressing a tell-tale smile, as he ushered her out of the door and down the street a little way. They passed houses at different stages of erection, with building rubble everywhere, until they stopped before a fan-shaped plot with only a concrete base protruding from the ground. The front garden was a normal rectangular shape, but the area at the rear was almost twice as wide as the house itself.

"Why have we stopped here?" she asked, puzzled at why he was keen to be showing her another stretch of concrete. "You're hiding something, aren't you?"

"Well," he started, "did you like the last show house we were in? The four bedrooms, the central heating, the—"

"And if I did?" she replied. "You know as well as I do that we have no chance of affording such a house. So why disappoint me when you know I would love it. All that space, and..."

"In six months' time," he said quietly and calmly, "with a bit of luck and good management, we will be moving into this one."

She fell silent, stared at the plot, as if envisaging the

house built and the garden set, and when she turned to Jack, tears were streaming down her face.

"It's cruel to have me on, Jack Ingles," she said, a puzzled frown crowding her face, "when you know—"

"Our name is on this one, Jenny," he nodded, "and the mortgage is settled. We move in six months or so from now."

"Central heating," she gasped, "a proper kitchen, and loads of space for the children inside and out. I can't believe it. You'll be telling me next that we're getting married tomorrow."

"As a matter of fact…" he grinned, raising his hands to ward off the handbag she would whizz over his head in fun.

"Are you sure we can afford it?" she asked once back in the car and on the road.

"Course we can," he replied. "Sorted. Be rayt. I made a promise to myself that if we ever got together, I would always try to make sure you had what you wanted, and this is part of that. Number 18 The Avenue."

"We haven't enough furniture to fill that house," she said, as the thought struck her. "We'll have to—"

"Make do until we can afford to change it," he added quite firmly.

"What you don't know, Jack," Jenny replied, staring him fully in the face before they set off to have a pub lunch at the John O' Gaunt, "is that I have more than a little cash put by from my dad's will which will see us with most of what we need."

"'Ark at you," he smiled. "Aren't you a dark horse? You'll be telling me next that you'll be buying yourself a new car."

"As a matter of fact—" she laughed.

"Touché," he yelled, joining in her sharp repartee. "You are so funny."

"Lunch, and then home to relieve your mam of her grandmotherly duties?" he suggested.

Chapter 17

"April seventh," Jack said, passing off his words as a nonchalant reminder at family breakfast on Sunday.

"April seventh what?" Jenny replied, as she helped little Jessie with her dippy boiled egg. She just had to have a dippy boiled egg and soldiers every Sunday breakfast. It had been a tradition religiously observed almost since the day she was born. It didn't matter that three quarters of the army always survived the campaign, along with almost all the egg.

"I don't know," he sighed, a wicked smile growing slowly. "Forgotten already? It's the day—"

"We are to be wed," she interrupted, clapping her hand to her mouth.

"Have we made any arrangements yet?" he asked, smiling sanctimoniously. "Apart from my having booked the registry office, that is."

"As a matter of fact," she replied, the smile returning to her lovely face, "they're on my 'to do' list for tomorrow, when you are at work."

"And that involves?" he asked, enjoying seeing how her mind worked. "Psychic activity? Telepathy?"

"Good old-fashioned paper and pencil planning, telephoning, and letter writing," she said, almost without thinking, as she finished Jessie's breakfast. "That will all be done by the time you get home. We'll be having the reception at either the Midland in t'Market Place, or t'Crown on Wakefield Road. As for—"

"Enough … enough," he pleaded, throwing his hands into the air. "Why did I doubt your organising skills?"

"We will talk about it tomorrow evening, naturally," she smiled as she cleared away and kissed him in passing.

"Do you feel like a walk to Newland Park in a bit?" Jack asked. "Bit of fresh air and sunshine?"

"Bit too far to walk for the girls, don't you think?" she said. "We could go by car and park there?"

"Good idea," he agreed, "if we can squeeze all their paraphernalia into our clapped-out shoe box, that is."

He used to play footy and have sports days on the fenced ground between the Catholic church and the park on Newland Lane when he was a nipper at Woodhouse. Just the other side of Newland Lane was the quarry that served Normanton Brickworks, and beyond that had been his granddad's rabbit trap run and his allotments. Their sports ground was only a rough and bumpy bit of a field with a set of goal posts at each end really, but it was all they had, because the land behind Woodhouse School was unfit.

This 'sports' ground also helped the school celebrate Summer Sports Day when his good mate, Trevor Durant, always won the sack race. He never jumped his sack to the winning post, risking falling in panicked haste. No. He stuck his feet in the sack's corners, and ran hell for leather towards the finishing tape. He always finished the race while everyone else was trying to sort out their feet from the pile they had left them in on the rough and uneven ground.

Newland Park wasn't big either, but it was reasonably well kept, and pretty in spring and summer.

"I used to come down here wi' mi mates," Jack said as they strolled through the park, "and we used to play at kick on the grass in the middle. We had to be careful because it was allus full o' dog muck – one of the reasons why I never brought my ball to play."

Ten minutes around the one path and they were out on Newland Lane again.

"Where does this road lead, Jack?" Jenny asked as they turned right.

"Carry on and I'll show you," he grinned.

Open fields, a railway line, a grass-covered slag heap, and … another brickworks dominated the view as they ambled around the lane. When they reached the railway bridge by Goosehill Junction, they stopped, as Jack's eyes glazed over.

"Penny?" Jenny ventured.

"Just here," he started, "ower this fence, me and mi pals used to sneak down the embankment to yon Wakefield Kirkgate line to watch the windshielders and streaks steaming past. Occasionally, we'd put a penny or ha'penny on the line to flatten it."

"We?" Jenny smiled.

"Well, not exactly we," he admitted. "I sat well back away from the line, for safety's sake, you understand. Didn't trust their judgement on timing."

"Too much of a risk, eh, Jack?" she said, knowing well what his reaction would be to anything unsafe or against the rules.

They ambled across the bridge just as a diesel passenger train chugged under their feet, barely causing any noise or vibration.

"We used to stand here many a time as a fast Fire Dragon screamed underneath," he went on, "covering us in smoke and steam, spitting sparks into our faces, and forcing an acrid sulphur stench up our nostrils. Fantastic."

"Fire Dragon?" she asked, casting a puzzled look at her man.

"It's what I used to call steam engines when I was a

nipper," he explained, a nostalgic smile crossing his lips.

"There's still a lot about you I don't know, my man," she said, linking his arm and drawing closer as he pushed the girls in their double Cindico Stroller pushchair. "And this was your playground? A road between open brickworks and a gigantic slag heap? What would you do here?"

"Fight a war, of course," he answered quickly, surprised that she couldn't see the potential for a group of young lads.

"A war?" she gasped. "Don't see what you would use hereabouts to even imagine you'd be able to … fight…"

"We used to come up here on a Sunday when the brickworks was shut," Jack started his tale, "wearing mi granddad's old ARP helmet and gas mask, and lob broken half bricks at each other, pretending they were grenades and you were enemies."

"Half bricks?" she asked incredulously. "I know I'm going to regret asking this, but where did you get them from?"

"What do you see across the road?" he pointed out, a smile on his face.

"Piles of bricks ready for … and lots of broken ones, scattered about," she said, realising with a wry smile. "Wouldn't that be dangerous, though?"

"Savage and brutal, war, owd love," he said making an obvious point. She laughed at the image of Jack as a nipper, wearing an ill-fitting helmet and frog-eye gas mask like some creature from the Black Lagoon, charging about 'killing' his enemies. "The muck heaps have a lot of fantastic fox holes and trenches to hide in to ambush unwary soldiers, you see."

"And when you had used all your grenades?" she asked.

"Unlimited supply ower yonder," he said, pointing to the neatly piled stacks of pristine new house bricks. "We'd just knock ower the odd few – all accidental like – and bingo, new supplies. You have to keep your supply lines open in war, you know. We'd been given several Scarborough warnings when they saw us, so that's why we moved to Sundays. Harmless fun."

They ambled back to the car, hand in hand, happy to be together, sucking in so many memories from Jack's childhood.

"I wish we'd been together then," he said wistfully, "you know, as pals."

"But your mates wouldn't have wanted me, a girl, as part of their gang," she smiled.

"Then, we would have been a gang of two," he replied quickly, and by the look on his face she could see how serious he was.

"You would have done that for me?" she said, drawing even closer to him, a look of love and respect in her eyes. "Jack and Jenny, the Two Musketeers. That would have taken the biscuit."

"As long as it was a digestive," he added, quick as a flash.

They laughed that laugh of happiness and freedom, as he wrapped his arms about her and drew her close, burying his face in her sweet-smelling hair, alive for just that one moment. He sighed deeply as he fumbled for the car keys.

"Can't find the keys," he said, turning out his pockets.

"They'll be in there somewhere," she said, "among the pieces of string, dried chewing gum, last year's conker, and a shiny pebble."

"How did you know?" he laughed. "Been through my pockets?"

"Not there," he said, a grunt of finality and concern sealing his rummage. "Sure you haven't got them?"

"Nowhere to put them," she insisted, spreading her arms wide. "I'll just have to look in the car, shall I?"

"But how can you, when—?" he said, as he was interrupted by the ominous click of an opening door.

"Oh," she laughed, "here they are ... on your seat, in the

corner."

"Wha—? How...?" he gasped. "How embarrassing is that? The car could have been stolen, or worse – it could have been left where it was."

-o-

Monday was never a good day to start work on, especially after a belting weekend. Jack didn't not like going to work, he simply felt there might – just might, mind – be a better way to pass the time. He had so much more 'stuff' he had to attend to. He had lots of unresolved issues whizzing around in his mind that he needed to find solutions for. So, he had to push them to the 'holding' area in his brain while he was in class.

Jenny, too, wanted him to be at home with her and the girls, not only because she didn't like them to be apart, but also because they had a lot to discuss and arrange regarding their impending nuptials.

Still, 1A– and 2A with his distant relative two hundred times removed – and fifth and sixth forms weren't too onerous a load for Monday.

"Don't you fancy having a go then?" Jim Stephenson asked Jack over their cup of morning break time tea.

"Having a go at what?" Jack said, through a mouthful of chocolate digestive. A slight smile of 'here we go again' began to turn Bill Jones' mouth at the corners. He had heard this question many times, and had even been asked himself. He had told Jim what to inflict upon himself, several times, but it hadn't stopped him asking.

"Doing an assembly, of course," Jim said, knowing what Jack's answer would be. Still, he had to try to involve the rank and file of the staffroom in his projects.

"What would it involve, Jim?" Jack asked.

"You don't have to apologise, it's ... What did you say?" Jim replied, sitting bolt upright and jerking a splash of tea down his suit front.

"I simply asked what I might be expected to do," Jack replied again. "If you aren't interested, I'll—"

"Hang on a mo," Jim interrupted him, quite surprised to receive a non-abusive response for once. "I didn't expect you'd be listening, let alone be interested."

"Who said I was interested?" Jack winked at Bill. "I simply want to know—"

"Choose your own topic," Jim responded quickly, feeling there might be mileage in pursuing this one. "A bit like John Crisp did last month, you know. Remember? The one he did about Vincent van Gogh. How you deliver it is up to you. Sky's the limit, really."

"Let me give it some thought, old chap," Jack said, smiling beatifically at the enthusiasm oozing from Jim's every pore, as he tried to persuade the younger man to have a go. Silence fell on the gathered throng as the young PE teacher-cum-rugby international, Iain MacManus strolled into the room, a puzzled look growing on his face.

"Don't worry, Iain," Ken Childs quipped, "it's not silent homage to you. Jack's just deciding whether or not to be persuaded to take one of Jim's assemblies. If he isn't, it'll be you next."

The five-minute bell interrupted all inconsequential chit chat, warning them that cups had to be emptied – either down throats or down the sink – washed and stacked before those on classroom duty trooped out.

"Jim," Jack called as he closed the door behind him. "You're on."

"Eh?" Jim said, surprised, almost choking on his last mouthful of lukewarm tea.

"I'll do it," Jack added. "Only, my choice, as it's getting closer, will be the Easter Story. You know? The full religious shebang."

"Wow," Jim gasped, a deeply surprised soft whistle

escaping his lips. "Go for it, Jack. You're a good man, and I'll—"

"Be forever in my debt?" Jack smiled. "I know. Don't forget. The full monty."

They left the staffroom corridor, Jim's friendly hand resting on Jack's shoulder, and a self-satisfied smile on his face.

"About time I did something around here to show I'm not just a pretty face," Jack laughed.

"You'll get no argument from me on that one, dear boy," Jim answered, satisfied with his job done.

-o-

Surprised not to see Jenny standing on the top step as he drew up to the front door, his Mini's exhaust coughing and spitting alarmingly, he unlocked the door and called, as he usually did.

"Jenny. I'm home."

"So am I," a little voice echoed as he spun around at a gentle touch to his shoulder.

"For goodness' sake!" he exclaimed, almost double somersaulting backwards off the top step. "That's another of my nine lives I won't get back. You scared me half to death."

He drew her into a hug and passionate kiss.

"It's a good job it was me, then," she laughed once he had surfaced for a breath, "with that sort of a kiss."

"I knew it was you straight away," he said, ducking the inevitable and completely expected cuff around the back of his head. "It was your heavy breathing that gave the game away."

"Cup of tea ready?" he joked, as they shut the door on the outside world.

"Mashing on the kitchen unit," she replied, a self-satisfied smile on her lips.

"Wouldn't a tea pot have been better?" he quipped. "Makes much less mess … I was joking. I didn't expect that reply, as you got home only fractionally after me. You are wonderful, Jenny Soon-to-be-Ingles."

"Did it before I scooted out for a mo to the corner shop," she replied. "I knew you'd be back at your usual time."

"Ever the psychic, my smart lady, eh?" Jack cracked as he poured the tea.

"Now," he started as they sat down for ten minutes' peace, "have…?"

"All done," she grinned, to see his look of puzzled surprise.

"All what?" he asked, testing her predictions.

"Wedding? Reception? Honeymoon?" she suggested.

"You mean—?" he said, taken aback by the speed of her organisation. "I thought you wanted to discuss the arrangements? You know, you … we?"

"No need," she answered cheerfully. "You were at work, and I had the time. I knew what we wanted, and everything fell into place. Boom. Boom. Job done."

"Come on, then," he urged, leaning back into the settee as he pulled her closer. "Tell me all about it."

"Well, first…" she started, her voice tailing away, as the fire cracked and spat in the grate.

Late March showers, though relatively short-lived, striped and rattled the window urgently, as if wanting to come in for a warm. A week away from the Easter holidays, nothing in their household seemed urgent, and yet…

"All arranged and in order," she said, rubbing her hands together. "Rarin' to go."

"Guests?" Jack asked.

"They've all known the date for weeks," she replied, "and all have replied – except for your brother."

"Why doesn't that surprise me?" Jack replied. "I won't ask again, so please don't remind them."

"Not going to happen, Jack," her tight-lipped reply came back quickly. "Val's my sister, and I would like her there, along with my niece and nephews. As for William? He can decide for himself."

Jack was quiet for a few moments, an irritated look lining his face. His annoyance wasn't directed at Jenny, though. His anger – and pity – were meant for his mean spirited and uncaring brother. These were traits Jack recognised from many years before.

"Joyce has said she wouldn't miss it for the world," she went on. "Unless, that is, her baby says otherwise."

"We should have around half a dozen to a dozen guests, then?" he said, a wry smile growing.

"Probably nearer to half, I think," she added, scratching her head. Shall we drag a few more in off the streets?"

"No bloody fear," he laughed. "Half a dozen'll do us fine, as long as it's all the ones as matter. Besides, cost'll be about rayt. As mi granddad would've said 'I'm not med o' brass.'"

-o-

"And as Jesus passed around the bread at the table of the last supper, he said…"

Jack's authoritative and compelling voice drew the rapt attention of his audience. They had all listened in silence – attentive, captivated by this young man's delivery of the well-known but little-understood Easter story, bringing a whole new meaning to their ignorant little lives.

The youngsters trooped out of the hall silently, out of respect for Jack, and reverence to the ethereal strains of the Easter Hymn from Cavalleria Rusticana in the original Italian, heralding the start of the last day but one of that particular term.

"Well," Jim Stephenson gasped as Jack collected his stuff together, "that was incredible, Jack. Thank you not only for doing the assembly, but for having the bravery and the brass neck to do that sort of religious assembly. It was immense."

"You're welcome, old chap," Jack replied, a huge grin stitching his ears together. "It was my pleasure, which I enjoyed thoroughly."

"Jack Ingles," Bill Jones started, as they entered the staffroom to begin their joint double free lesson, "when you get to be a headmaster, as you undoubtedly will with that sort of a masterful performance, please let me know. I should like to be a member of your staff."

"Thank you, sire," Jack said, bowing at his compliment. "Coming from you, that means a lot."

Chapter 18

"Last day as a free and single woman," Jack yawned as he turned over to kiss the lovely young lady lying beside him. "And then you become another of my chattels."

He didn't expect Jenny's reaction to his words, as she leaped on to him, straddling his chest and holding down his arms with her knees, while she tickled him in the only place he was ticklish – his neck.

Immediately, he became helpless and couldn't resist, as his laughter almost reached hysteria. Crying for mercy and begging forgiveness as tears rolled down his face, he was unable to move, even when she slid off his chest and skipped to the bathroom.

"You're a hard, unforgiving woman, Jenny-soon-to-be-Ingles," he gasped, wiping away the tears, and crawling on all fours to join her. "I am now exhausted and will be like a dish rag all day. How could you be so—?"

"Careful, chattel," she warned, laughter bubbling when she saw his prostrate body on the bathroom floor. "I can catch you any time, you know. Without warning I can strike when you are least expecting it. So, be careful. I don't forget."

"Neither do I," he guffawed, jumping from the floor to draw her into a clinch. As he took hold of her, he let out a cry of pain.

"Orgh!" he yelled, screwing his eyes and mouth shut

in silent anguish, as he fell to the floor again, grabbing his foot.

"What's the matter, love?" Jenny asked, a fleeting look of concern overtaking her face.

"Kicked the blasted toilet," he grimaced. "Think I might have broken mi little toe."

That fleeting look of concern lasted only a few seconds before she burst into uncontrollable fits of giggles, seeing her man sitting on the bathroom floor, naked, back against the bath, clutching his right foot.

"Not funny," he gasped, trying hard not to laugh. "I wouldn't put it past you to phone friends about this ... if we had any."

"I'm sorry," she said, trying to get her mirth under control, "but it was so funny seeing you hopping about trying to cradle your little toe, and trying not to let it show. Come on, my sweet, I'll put your socks on for you."

"Arrgh!" he yelled again, turning his back to her, trying valiantly to balance on one leg while gingerly feeding his injured foot through the leg of his underpants. "Don't you dare. I'll manage, thank you very much."

"Is it really that bad?" Jenny asked, worried that her hilarity had added to his demise. "I mean, I just thought it was ... funny, and you were putting it on to make me laugh ... more."

"'Fraid not, my lovely," he grimaced. "I would do anything to make you laugh, but breaking my bones is not one of them. Can't put my foot to the floor, so I don't know how I'm going to manage tomorrow."

"Oh, my God," Jenny exclaimed, slapping her hand to her mouth in shock. "What are we going to do? We can't put it off now, at this late time, can we?"

"No, we can't," he agreed, trying unsuccessfully to suppress a wicked snigger. "Just having you on."

"You ... you bugger," she shouted, landing out with the

damp towel in her hand.

"Well," he answered, "you laughed at my discomfiture when you thought I had broken my toe; my turn to laugh at your expense."

"Is it broken or not?" she asked, pulling him closer.

"Steady," he urged. "It is very sore, but I've no idea. They can't do anything other than tape it to the other toes, so I'll have to manage anyway. It should be OK by morning ... I hope."

"Then sit down and put your foot up," she ordered, ushering him towards the stairs.

"No chance," he replied, resisting. "Too much to do and too little time to do it in, my love. Be rayt. As long as I don't kick yon toilet again."

"Daft as a brush, some folk," she laughed. "Do anything for a bit of attention."

"Somebody at the front door," Jack shouted to her in the bathroom. "I'll get it."

Hobbling downstairs gingerly so as not to put too much pressure on his injured toe, he reached the door to find a note hanging through the letterbox, caught by a corner. He opened the door, and, peering both ways, could see nobody near. Scratching his head, he closed the door and slid open the note. Its contents surprised and concerned him deeply.

"Who was it, my lovely?" Jenny asked, as she slipped her arm around his waist. "Anybody important?"

"You need to see this," he said, handing her the hand-written note. "Brings a new dimension to our lives, I think."

"Well, the cheeky mare," she said, once she'd read its contents. "So, your ex-wife's back in the country, eh? And why do you assume that is, if her father's snuffed it? He must have left her suitably well cushioned, don't you think?"

"Money is what she wants," Jack said, as he tore up the note with suitable disdain. "She may have cash in the bank to buy somewhere suitably palatial, but she'll want a regular income to sustain my son until she gets a job."

"If she gets a job," Jenny said, a healthy dose of cynicism lacing her words. "Does this mean we won't be able to afford our house in Leeds?"

Seeing the panic beginning to imprint itself on her face, he drew her close to him and kissed the top of her head.

"Nothing's about to stop us buying our new home, my darling," he said adamantly. "We deserve that, and we'll bloody well have it as planned. Don't you fret about that."

"Mmm," she chuntered, looking up at him. "You sure?"

"Look at me," he insisted. "You've always said you could see my true thoughts and feelings in my eyes. Do you see capitulation and defeat there now? Do you?"

She put her arms around him, reached up to kiss him, and smiled that confident smile that trusted his words. She knew that Jack would rather die than break a promise.

"I love you, Jack Ingles," she murmured. "Time to push her out of our minds and focus on tomorrow."

"Why, what's happening tomorrow?" he asked in mock seriousness.

"Don't forget, O Ticklish One," she warned, a wicked gleam in her eyes, as she wiggled all her fingers, as if to grasp him, "that I can reduce you to a gibbering pile whenever I want."

He laughed as he kissed the top of her head, aware of the danger as he patted her bottom, and dodged into the kitchenette to prepare his masterly breakfast of porridge, fruit, tea, and … more tea.

Jenny couldn't imagine being any happier. Her two children were well-fed and content – the one gurgling in her crib in the corner of the lounge, playing with the sparkly mobile of animal figures strung across in front of her eyes; the other having a whale of a time by the front window. Jenny couldn't have been happier, marrying the man of her dreams the next day.

She stiffened as a knock on the door jerked her out of her dreams into the reality of a cool early April morning.

"Like bloody Briggate in her today. Get rid, Jen," Jack mouthed as he popped his head around the kitchenette door frame, "unless you want to share your next to last breakfast of freedom."

She unsnecked the door tentatively, and opened it a crack, not expecting to see…

"Val," she exclaimed. "Come in, love. Didn't expect to see you. William and the children?"

"Kids are at Mum's, but," she said, as she sucked in a deep intake of embarrassed breath, "otherwise … it's just me."

"William not coming, then?" Jenny asked, shrugging her shoulders in resignation. "We didn't think he would. Thank you for coming, though."

"It would have been sooner," she replied, "but we've only just finished for Easter – the kids and me."

"Porridge, Val?" Jack's voice attacked them from the kitchenette. "We're just about to eat. There's loads, and fruit a plenty."

"Well, go on then," she laughed, stripping off her outer layers. "It is a while since I ate and drank."

"Did you come over last night?" Jack asked as they settled to his most important feeding time of the day.

"This morning, very early," she replied. "The kids were barely awake. Made for a very peaceful journey, for once. I had forgotten how good your porridge was, Jack. Can I persuade you to come and make it for me? I could do with this every day."

"Any time, Val," he smiled. "For my favourite sister-in-law, any time."

"The last time I counted, my dear man," she laughed, "I was your only sister-in-law."

"Then you have joined the elite group of three females

whom Jack respects and reveres," Jenny said, as she slipped her spoon into her empty dish.

"Three?" Val asked, following suit.

"You, me," she continued, "and Jack's cousin, Irene."

"Do I know her?" Val queried. "Don't remember if I do."

"I don't think you've met yet," Jenny said, "but, if you're here for the wedding tomorrow, you will then. Are you?"

"Of course I am," Val harrumphed. "I wouldn't have missed it for all the tea in … Yorkshire."

"Ha ha ha …" Jack laughed. "All the tea in Yorkshire. Now, if that were real, I'd drink nowt else."

The coal in the grate crackled and spat, reminding him of similar times when he was a nipper at both Scarborough Row and Garth Avenue, as flames clawed their way up the fire back in their desperation to escape. He wished his mam could have been there to share in his happiness. She would have approved of Jenny, and of how she had brought happiness and contentment at last to her little boy, Jack.

"And William?" Jack asked quietly. "Why is he not coming to his brother's wedding?"

"He reckons he's too busy," she said, apologising for her husband's boorish and selfish behaviour, "and that you'll understand."

"Nothing I can do about that, then," he replied, after a moment or two's hesitation. "Anybody fancy a fresh pot of tea?"

The chorus of "Yes, please" followed him into the kitchenette.

"Jack seems to be taking his brother's attitude surprisingly well," Val said quietly to her sister.

"Don't you believe it," Jenny replied, hurt to think Jack's brother seemed not to care. "I know my Jack. He is very good at hiding stuff he has no control over. He will forgive – eventually, but he will never forget, and it will come back someday to bite William on the bum. The bonhomie on the surface hides a wealth of hurt, and feelings of betrayal and being let down."

"Anyway," Jenny went on, "how are things between you two – you know, after the last time you were here? Any change for the better?"

"Not really," Val said, a wry curl of the lip betraying how she felt about her husband's behaviour. "Jogging along in much the same sort of way. I don't know when it will all end – if ever it does."

"Val…" Jenny sighed, as she slid a supportive arm around her sister's shoulders.

"I'm not even sure we'll be together this time next year," she went on, tears springing to her eyes, and a single sob convulsing her shoulders.

"No," she insisted defiantly. "No. It's not going to happen. I won't let it."

"We're here whenever you need us," her sister reassured her quietly.

"We certainly are," Jack agreed, as he emerged from the kitchenette, a fresh pot of tea and a plate of chocolate digestives on a tray.

"Jack, surely not," Jenny burst in, a grimace on her face. "Not chocolate digestives, surely. We've still got the taste of porridge in our mouths. Do we—?"

"There is no definitive time when a chocolate digestive should be consumed," he insisted. "As long as it is accompanied by a fresh, hot mug of tea, that's the only criterion for its appearance on the menu. Now, when do we get to see our niece and nephews?"

Chapter 19

The ante-room to the registry office was cool, even at a quarter to midday. Two small, low tables gathered several orderly easy chairs around them, waiting for their first joyous, nervous customers of the day. Although outwardly the building was beginning to betray its age, the authority responsible for its upkeep had tried to maintain at least a semblance of the modern within its meagre means.

Vases of freshly-cut flowers decorated both tables, and modern paintings in keeping with impending events adorned the walls. Everything around, including the front of house staff, exuded cheerfulness and joy.

Quarter to noon was the agreed meeting time for Jenny and Jack's celebration of their union after what seemed like an eon of waiting – their time when nothing was going to intrude to throw the event off balance.

"You look lovely, Joyce," Jack said to his long-time friend, as she struggled to sit in the easy chair he had just vacated for her. "Baby not far away, eh?"

"Anything up to a week," she replied, a slight grimace of discomfort hijacking her face as she rearranged her bump gently.

"I am really grateful you came," he said, shaking John's hand warmly. "Fire and the other emergency services are on standby, just in case."

Joyce laughed.

"Yes, you always were funny, Jack Ingles, even at Woodhouse Nursery," she added. "Although, sometimes I wasn't sure it was intended."

"Irene … David," Jenny smiled, as she hugged them both. "Thank you for coming. It's good to see you. How's little Olivia Rose?"

"Good to be here," Irene replied. "She's fine and is with David's mum, as is Jessie."

"Irene … David," Jack said, greeting his cousin and his good friend. "You will be able to stay for the reception, I hope? Only … it's not every day you have the head of your old school acting as a witness at your wedding."

"Of course we will, old man," David grinned, "but it's back to being ordinary deputy again, I'm afraid. CPB's returned from illness, more chipper than ever. Still, it was good experience, and he said it shouldn't be too long before I get a permanent billet of my own."

"I always knew you were going far," Jack guffawed. "The—"

"Further the better," David joined in, bursting out laughing with him. "I do miss our aging repartee."

Midday chimed on the local church clock.

The partition door opened as a large lady in a voluminous lime green dress and black bolero jacket drew their attention.

"The Ingles party, if you please," she announced, her shrill voice rattling around the false low polystyrene ceiling. "Mrs Miller, the registrar, is ready for you now."

"It's a shame your gran couldn't be here, Jack," Val said as she trooped through the ceremony room with her brood.

"She's not very well at the moment, sadly," he replied. "I know it's still raw, but she can't get mi granddad out of her mind. She talks to him a lot these days. We just have to get on with it."

"You all right, Joyce, love?" her husband whispered in

her ear, as he noticed the ashen look on her face. "Baby?"

"Aye, lad," she answered quietly. "Just jumpin' about a bit, that's all. I'll be all rayt. No need to fuss."

The room fell silent as Jenny and Jack and their six adult guests and an age spread of five children shuffled into their semi-circle of seats before the registrar's huge desk.

"Would the happy couple and their witnesses please approach the desk?" Mrs Miller said, a cheerful smile welcoming the gathered throng.

"Mummy?" Mary asked Val in an audible whisper.

"Yes, my pet," Val said, expecting the worst. "What is it?"

"I need to—" Mary started.

"Not now, sweetie," her mother whispered back. "You'll have to hold it until—"

"But I need to move seats now," she said, her insistent whisper muffled because of her pinched nostrils. "Edward's pumped again, and the smell's awful."

"Gathering together to celebrate the joining…" the registrar's voice continued its liturgical drone, trying its best to instil a certain mystique into the proceedings.

"But Mum—" Mary's insistent, hoarse whisper protested.

"Do you Jack take—?"

"You sure you're all right, Joyce?" John insisted. "You don't look at all—"

"Husband and wife together—"

"You'll need to see I get to the ladies," Joyce whispered urgently to her husband. "I think—"

"Jack and Jenny Ingles. You may kiss—"

"The baby's head," Joyce urged as quietly as she could, given how she was feeling. "I think it's about to pop out."

Joyce struggled to her feet, supported by her husband, and waddled slowly towards the partition door. Everyone was focused on Jack and Jenny signing the register and taking photographs – everyone except for Val, who recognised the signs of imminent birth in such a heavily pregnant woman.

"Edward and Joey," she whispered to her boys, "sit still here and look after your sister. I'm looking for you both to be grown-up now. I'll be back in a jiffy."

Semi-stooped and as unobtrusively as she was able, Val crept out of the room to follow Joyce and John to the toilets, where they arrived at about the same time. Obviously, Joyce's waters had broken, and she was bent almost double in pain, already pushing instinctively.

"Nearly here, Joyce?" Val suggested. "Quick! Into the toilet – and you, John, phone for an ambulance. Don't worry. I'll look after her. By the time you're back, you'll probably be a father, so you'll need to stop anyone coming in. Hurry."

"Where's Joyce?" Jenny said to her husband of two minutes. "And Val? Oh, my God. You stay here, Jack. I think she might be dropping yon young 'un. Gather everybody in the other room … and keep them there."

"Mrs Miller," Jenny whispered to the registrar, "may I have a word?"

"Of course," she replied once she had realised the urgency of the situation. "I'll come straight away. I used to be a midwife. I'll grab some towels from my rest room, and—"

-o-

"Well, that was fun," Jack said to Joyce, as she saw to her new addition in the hospital ward. "She's gorgeous."

"I'm so sorry—" she started to apologise.

"Don't you dare, Joyce Walker," Jenny insisted. "You have nothing to be sorry for. It almost came off."

The four of them laughed, as Joyce nursed her little scrap of humanity.

"Is everything – you know – all right?" Jack asked tentatively.

"Aye. Course it is," Joyce replied. "Right as rain. Overnight stay is all we need, to keep an eye on t'vitals and stuff. Then Stick here comes in t'mornin' to bring us home."

"Stick ... ha ha," Jack guffawed. "That's funny ... Stick."

"Well, that's allus been his name, ant it?" she smiled. "Well, it is now."

"Even though it didn't turn out quite like we'd planned," Jack said, taking Joyce's hand, "we are really grateful you came. Unfortunately, neither of you got to enjoy the reception at the Crown, but Jenny has boxed you up some stuff from the buffet though, so you shouldn't starve."

"Fantastic," Stick said, pleased that they'd got to eat at last. "We've not had owt since breakfast. I'll go and see if I can rustle up some tea."

"You do realise, of course," Joyce said, as she was unpacking the box of goodies Jenny had brought, "that mine was the quickest first baby delivery on record?"

"Quick Draw McWalker, eh?" Jack quipped, as they all laughed.

"My second was all of fifteen hours," Jenny added, a grimace of remembrance flicking over her face. "Much longer than with Jessie, and not at all comfortable, I can tell you."

"I don't remember much about the affair," Joyce continued, "except for the help your Val gave me. I would have been in a serious mess if she hadn't followed me out and taken charge. Could you thank her again, please, and let her know that we intend to call our little miracle Valerie?"

"Wow," Jenny gasped, overcome by this. "Val will be so pleased, and no doubt overcome by your gesture. She's at Mum's with her brood, and will be returning to the Midlands day after tomorrow."

"Will you bring them all round to ours tomorrow," Joyce asked, "so I can thank her personally, and her kids for being so well-behaved?"

"When Baby and I were taken out to the ambulance, though," Joyce went on, "there was a man hanging about by the registry office, who looked singularly like your dad, Jack. When he saw me looking, he dodged around the corner very sharpish, and wasn't to be seen when we set off."

Jack was quiet, not wanting to allow himself to become angry. After all, he hadn't bothered any of them, and wasn't part of their day. Although Jenny's attitude towards him was a lot softer and more placatory than Jack's, he would never be part of their life. Jack would never let him back in ever again.

Jenny noticed the hardening of his face at what Joyce had said, realising that, although there was an outward steely shell about him, there would be a serious struggle going on in his head between pragmatism, conscience, and compassion. She was quite sure which would win.

They left Joyce and John in the ward, tucking in to their 'reception meal', looking every inch the doting parents of their daughter Valerie. They wished they could have spent more time with Irene and David, but they had had to get back to rescue Mrs Aston from her dutiful babysitting. Next time they would plan to spend more time together – the whole extended clan.

"We'll do that when we move into our new four-bedroomed palace," Jenny said, squeezing Jack's arm as they headed for the car. "Enough space for them to stay over and spend some time letting our kids get to know one another. When will we be able to move in?"

"Probably the end of August, I think," he said, plucking a month out of the air. "Or September … or October … or…"

"OK," she sighed. "I get it. Let's go home, eh?"

Although technically and meteorologically early spring, there was still an edge of winter about this early evening. However, the extra hour's daylight recently acquired had begun gradually to wrestle and loosen winter's grasp on the year. The translucence of the dark brought hope and cheer that more clement conditions were just around the corner.

Heath Common slid past in silence, except for an ominous rattle on the exhaust that Jack prayed was simply a loose bracket. Pineapple Hill had always been a trial for this dodo of a car, but lately the engine had begun to protest more vehemently. He hoped that this day wasn't the day it said "Enough. Can't do this anymore."

Thirty miles an hour became fifteen, and then five, as they struggled to the crown of the hill.

"Come on, you old bucket," Jack muttered, as the new road opened up in front of them. "Downhill from here. Come on."

"Problems, husband?" Jenny asked, eyes opening finally after a short nap.

"Nothing a new engine wouldn't solve," a wry grin telling the full story. "Oh, and add a reasonably new body to that as well."

Picking up speed slowly again, Jack released a slow hiss of relief that they weren't about to spend their honeymoon night in this Mini on Wakefield Road, near to the house they had almost bought. That would have been bitter irony indeed.

"Cup of tea, Mrs Ingles?" Jack asked once they had snecked the door.

"Too right, Mr Ingles," Jenny replied. "Can I tempt you to a digestive to go with that?"

"You can tempt me to anything, my beautiful wife," he replied with a wickedly suggestive grin. "You know I can resist anything but temptation."

"Digestive first," she laughed, "then suggestive afterwards. OK?"

"Can't believe we've finally gone and done it," Jenny sighed as she joined Jack on the settee.

"Finally managed what I should have done years ago," he replied, digestive crumbs forming a ridiculous moustache on his top lip. "Something I shall never forgive myself for."

"Jack," she sighed. "We've done it, and that's all that matters."

"I promise you, Jenny Ingles," Jack started after a moment's thought, "that I will look after you and make you happy for the rest of your life."

"You had me the day you walked through my door, Jack," she smiled, "and today cemented it."

"Shall we go and fetch the kids from your mum's place?" he asked. "She has been overflowing for a while."

"Yeah," she replied, "and then we can get back to normal married life. However, I do think we might need an early night."

-o-

"Jenny," Jack shouted after ten minutes outside. "It'll have to be a walk. Car won't start."

Chapter 20

"I'm afraid you'll have to rethink your plans, Mr Ingles," Jack Beddowes apologised as he handed back Jack's car keys.

"I don't understand," Jack muttered, scratching his head whilst trying to figure out what he was saying. "Are you saying that it's going to cost me to have it fixed, or are you saying you can't fix it?"

"The latter, I'm afraid," Mr Beddowes replied, shrugging his oily overalls and shaking his head. "The only place that car's going is the scrapper."

"But you're a mechanic," Jack protested, "and mechanics can do anything, can't they?"

"That's very true, within reason," Mr Beddowes said calmly, "but there is a bit of a difference between mechanic and magician, I think. I'll give you a tenner for it. Otherwise, you'll have to take it away yourself, but it's not … working."

"Deal, Mr Beddowes," Jack said, offering his hand in a gesture of acceptance. "Bit of advice, please?"

"Shoot," the mechanic agreed.

"I need a motor to transport mi family," Jack started. "What sort of a saloon should I go for, and how much might it cost? Not too costly, preferably. Doesn't have to be a Rolls Royce."

"Well," he replied, "if I were you, I'd go for a Vauxhall Viva. Solid car, twelve hundred cc engine – agreed, it's a bit underpowered, but it will get you reliably from A to B. Cost new? About a thousand; perhaps eleven hundred? We could get you one, but it would cost you a bit more."

"How much more?" Jack came back quickly.

"Another ton on top," the mechanic said, but straight away the young man's face told him he wouldn't go for that.

"No skin off my nose, but the main dealer in the area is Wallace Arnold on Roseville Road in Leeds. They will deliver at a cost of twenty pounds.

"And how would I do that when I've no transport?" Jack sighed, patting the now scrapped Mini.

"Train and bus will cost you a sight less than hiring one of my cars for the day," Mr Beddowes replied, "but it's your choice. I know what I'd do."

"Train and bus?" he ventured.

"Too right," the mechanic replied, nodding sagely.

"Thank you," Jack said. "You've been very honest, and the tenner will go towards…"

His voice tailed away as a hefty chill wind eddied around the forecourt. He remembered being captivated as a nipper by the smell of the petrol pumps, and that one sniff was enough as he passed through, on his way to the undulating field behind his grandma's house. Two derelict air raid shelters, some hills and valleys to hide in, a lot of long grass, and – joy of all joys – a largish pond. Not as big as Goosehill fields pond, by any means, but big enough to fall into and get covered in mud.

Those were the days.

Many's the time he'd taken a header into its shallows, and stood silently on his back step at home waiting for his mam to blast him out about being covered in mud and pond weed. But she never did. She'd call him a 'muck lump', strip him off on the top concrete step, stuff his mucky clothes into the copper in its wash house (in the days before their English Electric washing machine with its vertically central agitator), and usher him to the bath upstairs to be scrubbed clean.

His bath day had always been Sunday, at four, but his encounter with the pond always gave him an extra bath, much to his disdain. Once bathed and changed, he wasn't allowed to go out again, no doubt to get mucky once more. This had always been a bone of contention for him, because the other nippers were allowed out until seven, but he would never say.

"Roseville Road, you say?" Jack reiterated, as he turned to leave.

"A tenner for you love," he shouted, as he locked the front door. "Mrs Ingles ... pay day!"

"Is that all I'm worth after last night?" she grinned. "Don't you dare say you need change."

They laughed as they settled on the settee with a cuppa, and a reassessment of their finances.

"So, what do we do now, Mr Ingles?" she asked, knowing what his answer would be. "Any ideas?"

"If we buy a second-hand car," he explained, "not only will it cost us in repairs and servicing, but we'll have to replace it that much more quickly."

"Quicker than what?" Jenny asked, knowing very little about the whys and wherefores of car purchase.

"Than if we buy something new but reasonably cheap," he replied. "We're not talking a Mark Ten Jaguar here."

"So, what are we talking?" she asked. "We certainly don't want another Mini."

"Mr Beddowes at the garage gave me some advice," Jack said. "He'd no axe to grind because they don't sell them – but he suggested we go for a new Vauxhall Viva Deluxe, which will give us enough space for our present family, with reliability for the next few years."

"How much?" she asked.

"About a grand, give or take," he replied, "but we would

have to go to Leeds to get one."

"Why Leeds, for goodness' sake?" Jenny said, not understanding why there wasn't one anywhere nearer.

"Well," he replied, "it doesn't have to be. He says he could get one for us, but it would cost more. So…"

Jenny loved to watch his face as he explained things to her. He was so precise in every detail, that, part way through she often lost track. That didn't matter, however, because he always explained it in at least three different ways, anyway.

"And that would see us right for a year or two," he finished. "We'll have to do hire purchase though, because the money I saved has all but gone, save a bob or two that we need to keep back for eventualities."

"Mine hasn't," she added, a smile on her face as she snuggled closer to him.

"Yours hasn't what?" he puzzled.

"The money Dad left me will more than amply cover that," she explained, "with plenty to spare."

"But," he began to protest, "that's for—"

"Us to use where and when we see fit," she replied, emphasising 'we'. "Dad left me that money to make life that bit more comfortable for Jessie and me, and now I have Florence May and Jack to add to my collection. We need transport to make our collective lives that bit easier, so boom boom. Job's a good un, as your—"

"Granddad would say," he finished, a laugh bubbling up. "Well said, the lady in the red trousers."

"So, how and when are we to get this … machine?" She added, genuinely having no idea. "I don't feel too much like traipsing to Leeds. Do you?"

"The only way we can do it then," he replied, "is through Beddowes' Garage, and they charge a hundred pounds on top."

"Price we have to pay, then, I suppose," she answered, matter-of-fact. "How about nipping down to see the man now, then, and hopefully we might be mobile before too long? It's what the money's for."

-o-

"Val?" William said, walking into the lounge at the end of his working day, and seeing his wife sitting in his favourite chair. "Children not in?"

She lifted her eyes from the magazine pages she was flicking, to fix his face as he stood before her.

"They are with my friend, Jeannie, for a while," she started. "We need to talk."

"Any chance of a cup of tea?" he asked, nervously, feeling an atmosphere as he wondered what he had done wrong.

"Fresh in the pot," she replied, turning back to her magazine nonchalantly, and without ostensible emotion. She steadied herself and waited for his return.

"What do you want to talk about?" he said, as he set his mug on the coffee table next to his favourite chair. "Problem with the kids?"

"We need to talk about Samantha, William," she said, dropping the magazine to the floor, and fixing her gaze on his eyes. That one name gave her the reaction she had anticipated, but had wanted not to see.

"Samantha?" he said, trying to appear cool and in control. "Samantha who?"

"Don't try to play clever with me," she said, an uncharacteristically aggressive attitude taking over. "I know about the other life you've been leading for God knows how many months. I don't wish to go into the unseemly details of your sordid little affair, but at least do me the courtesy of not insulting my intelligence."

This stopped him in his tracks as he slumped into his chair, chin resting on his chest.

"I didn't mean it to happen, Val," he admitted, "but—"

"Don't you 'Val' me," she interrupted angrily, but toning

down the outburst almost immediately. "You have two options. You end it immediately ... if not for my sake, for the good of your children."

"And the other option?" he asked, finally engaging her gaze.

"You're out of our lives completely," she replied, tight-lipped. "You're not messing us about. You either put us first, or you move out to be with your whore, and we return to Yorkshire and the family that does care about us. History repeating itself, eh?"

"How do you mean?" he said quietly. "I don't understand."

"Like father, like son?" she said. "And you had the audacity to pitch against your brother. You are something of a hypocrite, I'd say. He's twice the man you'll ever be."

A sneaky silence slipped into the room unnoticed, killing all communication between them. Neither had wanted this confrontation, and neither would allow it to remain, for the sake of their children.

"I'm going to pick up Joey, Edward and Mary now," Val said quietly, a tear glistening the corner of her eye, knowing that it would betray her feelings, but hoping it didn't, "and I want no more mention until you've sorted things out. Don't think, either, that this lets you off the hook. It'll take a long time for me to get over this, if I ever do."

-o-

"What are you doing here at this time?" Samantha said, panic setting in on seeing William standing before her door. "My husband will be here in an hour with the kids."

"It's urgent," William said, sidling into the hall. "Val's found out about us, and I've been given an ultimatum that—"

"I know," she interrupted.

"I ... You know—?" he stopped in mid-sentence. "How could you know?"

"I just ... do," she replied. "It's what I thought was going to happen, but we must continue as we agreed."

"Well," he went on, "we can't."

"Can't?" Sam said, astounded by his attitude. "Can't? But, I thought you wanted to be with me."

"I do," he insisted, "but it means I will lose my kids, if we're together."

"And they're more important than me?" she hissed, becoming emotional at what she was hearing. "I'm prepared to lose my kids, and you tell me we can't? Besides, we can't separate now."

"Why?" he puzzled. "I don't understand—"

"Well, you'll bloody well have to," she insisted, tears welling in her eyes. "I'm pregnant."

"Pregnant?" he mouthed, the word hitting him like a sledge hammer between the eyes. "But ... you ... can't ... be."

"I can," she interrupted, "and ... I ... am."

"But are you sure?" he said in a panic, and trying to find a way out. "You know ... that it's—"

"Don't you bloody dare," she screeched. "You bastard. Of course it's yours. I know it's yours. Do I need to spell it out? Do I need to tell you that you're the only person I've had sex with over the last six months?"

By this time she was beside herself, with anger and emotion overflowing like a dam burst, and nothing he could do would repair the damage his size ten boots had done.

"Go," she said, bursting into deep heart-felt sobs. "Just go."

William turned, mind numb and heart heavy after what he had thoughtlessly inflicted on the woman wanted to be with, but giving no thought to the woman at home who loved him and with whom he had been through so much.

What had he done?

He had relegated his wife of ten or so years to an also-ran, when she should have been his priority.

He had done some dumb things in his life, but this was not his finest hour.

Chapter 21

The summer term in school petered out in no especially exciting way. The only microcosmic disturbance had been a two-week teachers' strike ordered by his union in protest against the usual two demons – pay and conditions. Jack refused to strike on principle and was summarily drummed out of the second largest teachers' union at the time. This didn't faze him at all because nobody, let alone a pettifogging teachers' union, was about to compromise his principles.

The school was closed for that length of time and so he had to report daily to the education offices to prove he wasn't getting an extra paid holiday, courtesy of his colleagues. Their attitude to his blacklegging was mixed, however. Some of his closer colleagues understood and supported his philosophical stand, but others ostracised him because of his principles.

The end of term couldn't come soon enough for him.

Moving-in day for their new house in North Leeds had been set for the week after breaking-up day, and they were counting down eagerly. The cost of the new car had had to come out of Jenny's inheritance, leaving that much less for new furniture, but that didn't concern her.

"We've got more than enough furniture for the new house," she would say, when the conversation turned round to the removal, which it did virtually every day.

"This porridge, Jack, is—" Jenny said at breakfast early on Removal Day.

"Delicious? Delectable? Divine?" he interrupted, in a highly good mood.

"OK," she laughed.

"OK? OK," he guffawed. "A good, large meal to sustain all our efforts on this very important and auspicious day. We—"

"All right. All right," she laughed. "We're moving to Leeds, not Downing Street."

A light tap at the door stopped them in mid-chew. Casting puzzled looks at each other and shrugging shoulders, Jenny got up to answer.

"Val?" Jenny puzzled, ushering her sister into the house. "Seems like an obvious question, but what are you doing here?"

"A little bird told me you were doing something momentous today," she smiled. "Now, what was it? Oh, yes. You're moving house, and I thought you might need some help."

"Very kind of you," Jack said. "Had breakfast? Help yourself to porridge. There's a scrap left in the pan."

"It's all right," she replied, sitting down and pouring a cuppa. "I've eaten at Mum's."

"William and the kids here too?" Jenny asked, guessing what the likely answer might be.

"He's at home," she replied, pulling a face, "looking after the kids."

"Not spending too much time together lately, then?" Jack asked pointedly, as might have been expected from him.

"One or two 'issues', I'm afraid," she said. "I'll explain later."

The removal van rattled to a halt outside the front door of number 18 in good time, ready to haul all their worldly belongings off to North Leeds and their new palace. They didn't have much, so it took the removal men all of thirty-two minutes to draw down and secure their tail gate shutter doors.

"We'll be off, then, missus," the driver said. "It'll teck us abaht an hour and a arf to get yonder, if that's all rayt wi' you?"

"Thank you, Mr Penny," she replied, shuffling into the back of their champagne-coloured chariot, next to their Val, as an excited frisson overtook her from top to toe. "See you there at about midday then."

"Electricity and gas are off, and meters read," Jack began, as he scrambled into the driving seat. "The house is empty and the doors are locked. Now for the open road, a book of verse, and a light to shine the way."

"He always says that, Val," Jenny laughed. "It's a ritual he can't seem to do without."

"Damn," Jack cursed, as he turned right into the High Street by Womack's florist on the corner opposite Woolworth's. "Do you know what we've not packed?"

"Oh, no," groaned Val.

"Don't forget I know you of old, husband," Jenny said, a knowing smile creasing her eye corners. "Absolutely nothing."

"Correct," he agreed.

"Like I said," Jenny continued. "Same rigmarole every time."

Turning the corner left past the Black and White Swan pubs for the last time, they purred down Castleford Road past Haw Hill Park, Beckbridge estate, and the Common Junior School – on towards Whitwood. The hill up to the Four Lane Ends roundabout near the college was always a slow one, giving him time to swing left to head out to the River Calder, the countryside beyond, and to Methley.

They had finally left Normanton behind; that important

little town that had spawned, educated, and guided them towards the life they wanted to pursue.

Good old Normy!

"Do you ever have any regrets about leaving?" Jenny asked Val, as they sped along Barnsdale Road past Pinfold Lane where Jack had celebrated many a victorious rugby match courtesy of Methley Rugby Club's glorious grounds. Their Saturday evenings' celebrations often revolved around bottled Newcastle Brown Ale supped at the Plough Inn, Warmfield. It was wonderfully exciting how a street name could discharge a myriad glorious memories with just one split second's glance.

"Occasionally, yes," Val replied, a moment's thought later. "I love the house we live in now, despite the amount of work that needs to be done to it both inside and out. William's not a DIY person – never has been – and he says we can't afford to have someone in to do the work."

"Always was a lazy sod," Jack butted in. "Could never see beyond his nose end."

"Jack," Jenny hissed, astounded at his forthrightness. You could always rely on him to put in his honest ha'pworth at an inappropriate time.

"What?" he asked in mock surprise. "Just saying."

"He's right, of course," Val agreed. "He's always wanted an easy life. Always wanted the kids to fit into a mould, for example. Usually left discipline and their management to me, while he did the fun things with them. Lovely Daddy!"

"This brings back memories," Jack said, once they were on Leeds Road. "This little area ower yonder to the right, is called John O'Gaunt, and yon pub bearing the same name, was run by the parents of a mate of mine. Just over the rise going on towards the railway line, is a little muck-covered lane called Pickpocket Lane. We had many a good time making up stories about what might have happened there."

"Mate of yours?" Jenny puzzled. "How could he be a

mate when you lived in Normy, and he lived out ... here?"

"Because—" Jack began to answer, deliberately.

"He moved from Normanton for his folks to take over at the pub?" she said, realising straight away she had been a bit hasty to interrupt.

"Exactly," he said, smiling at her flashbulb moment.

"Is William's way part of the problem, do you think, Val?" Jenny asked.

"I suppose it is, really," she said, a wistful look clouding her eyes. "That and the affair he's been having."

Now, that was a conversation-stopper to end all conversation-stoppers.

"Affair?" Jenny gasped, finding sufficient words finally to express her disdain and disbelief. "How long's that been going on?"

"About six months, as far as I can gather," she replied dismissively. "Can't get too much out of him."

"Wow," Jack hissed. "I was going to say I'm shocked, but I'm really not. He always was secretive, but not cleverly enough so that I couldn't see through him, even at seven."

"But, why?" Jenny said, still not able to believe it of him. "It's not as if you're a bad wife and mother – he couldn't have done better—"

"It looks like he thinks he could," Val interrupted quietly, withdrawing almost within herself. "Anyway, he's had my ultimatum. Get rid of her, or we're moving back here."

"We?" Jack asked, not sure what to expect.

"The kids and me," she replied, forcefully, very determined to show she could be strong. "He will be history, and we will take him for everything we are entitled to."

"Although he is my brother, Val," Jack said quietly, as he turned right on to Crown Point Road, aiming for Regent Street and the A61 north, "I have to say, we are one hundred per cent behind you. If we can help in any way – in any way, mind you – don't hesitate to ask."

"Thank you, Jack," she replied. "You are a good man, but I hope it won't come to that."

"Look over to your left, Jenny," he urged, slowing down slightly. "This is Roseville Road, and that main car dealership over there is where this car came from."

"Oh, nice," she replied, dispassionately. She wasn't a car person, so a car was just … a car to her, and it was of no relevance whether it came from Roseville Road or Roseville, Minnesota.

"I hope you won't have to bring it back here if anything goes wrong with it," she said dismissively.

Roundhay Road and Prince's Avenue took them past North Park Avenue where he lived as a young teacher, and where his cousin Irene had swung back into his orbit once again.

"This is where I used to live when I first came out of college," he reminisced, "and where Irene came back into my life. The kids are going to have such a fantastic time with Roundhay Park so close to where we will be living. Can't wait to show them around…"

"And…?" Jenny reminded him.

"And you, of course, Mrs Ingles," he added quickly. "It wouldn't be any fun without you."

"You lived around here with your first wife, didn't you?" Val asked.

"Don't remind me," he said gruffly. "It was OK when we were on our own, but then her father appeared on the scene, and everything fell apart from there. Not a happy time in my life."

"And what happened to turn it around?" Jenny reminded him with her usual poke in the back.

"Cemetery," he replied, turning into a new housing estate.

"But this is a—?" Val said, confusion covering her face.

"Housing estate," he added quickly. "I know. Our housing estate. However, it was a chance meeting in Normanton Cemetery that turned my life around. Remember, Val? Your visit to ascertain our intentions?"

"Of course," she laughed. "Mum's friend saw you kissing in the graveyard."

"The most important event of my life," he said with a grin of enormous satisfaction. "Well, we're here."

He pulled into a long wide driveway, which led to what seemed to be a palatial new detached house. The removal van was nowhere to be seen as yet, but the most worrying thing was that the house doors were locked.

"I'd better nip up to the site office and see about some keys," Jack threw over his shoulder as he trudged up the site to find the agent.

"Be sharp, Jack," Jenny called after him. "Removal van's just rounding the bottom bend now."

"'Fraid we can't get in, Mr Penny," Jenny said to the driver as they pulled up. "The site agent's not seen fit to welcome us to our new home."

"Jack's on his way back now, Jen," Val noticed, tapping her sister on the shoulder, "and he's got an official-looking man with him."

"Had to wait for a phone call from head office," Jack started, "to verify the money from our solicitor had been transferred. Fortunately, Mr Smith here sharpened them up ... and now here we are, about to enter our new home."

"Blooming heck!" Val gasped as they sat round the dining table, ready to tuck into the sandwiches and two flasks of tea Jenny had made. "This house is enormous."

"Probably because we don't have much furniture to clutter it," her sister retorted with a snort.

"Even so," Val replied, "it is big, and the garden—"

"Will need a lot of work," Jack answered as he slid into the table beside his wife, "but I'm looking forward to doing it myself."

"We will do it together," Jenny butted in sharply. "Couple of wide borders, an island bed or two in a large green lawn ... heaven."

"And who's going to buy us a mower?" Jack asked. "We can't borrow your mum's. It's too far away."

"We will, my dear Percy Thrower, and you will mow," she smiled, "and I will sow to make the garden grow for our little Flo."

"For goodness' sake, don't give up the day job," he urged, laughing at her feeble attempt at rhyme.

"This affair, Val," Jack asked, as he started his second digestive, "how did you get to know?"

"A little bird," she replied, a weak smile escaping.

"A little bird you know well?" Jenny joined in. "Someone close?"

"Suffice it to say it was a close friend who had seen them leaving a hotel together when he should have been elsewhere," Val added carefully. "I know it's a bit of a stretch from the one thing to that far-reaching assumption, but several other things suddenly gelled together in my mind, setting off alarm bells. I did a bit of digging myself, and was able to put two and three together—"

"To make five," Jack whooped. "My saying from when I was seven."

"Mary's saying now, too," she smiled. "She has a lot of your traits, does my Mary."

"Then she is a true Ingles," he agreed, as they all laughed.

"Wait-and-see time, then," Jenny said, ending that conversation. "So, when will we have the pleasure of a family visit to our new abode?"

"Any time, Val," Jack interrupted. "Just ... not tomorrow."

"It will be either four or five of us," Val replied, "depending on circumstance and the outcome from my ultimatum ... and hopefully, that will be soon."

Chapter 22

"I really, really love this house, Jack," Jenny said, snuggling up to him in bed a couple of weeks after moving in. "Thank you for what you've given me."

"What are you thanking me for?" he said, furrows lining his brow. "I've done nothing."

"No, of course you haven't," she replied, sarcastically. "Had it not been for you coming back to me – Jessie and me – we would still have been in Normanton, lonely, and not in this lovely – beautiful – big new house. That's all."

"And, without you, I would no doubt still have been living in a bedsit in Roundhay," he said. "So less of that then, eh? We are what we are, and we've both been fortunate."

"I hear and obey, O masterful husband," she mocked, a wickedly mischievous grin on her face. It was at times like this Jack had to be on his guard, because he never knew what she might do. Her favourite manoeuvre was to lull him into a false sense of security by feigning getting up, and then leaping on to him, her tickling fingers flicking and clicking like miniature helicopter blades.

He then had to deploy his cunningly conceived counter measures, which really amounted to his superior strength, to prevent her closing in on his ticklish neck. Once she had broken through that line of defence, however, he was helpless, and she could tickle him until tears rolled down his helpless face.

"Fancy visiting your mum today?" he asked, as he brushed his teeth in the large new-fangled en suite sink, keeping an eye over his shoulder at all times. "I wouldn't mind taking her for lunch to the Plough, and then a round trip ride to Kirkthorpe, the Half Moon Lake, Heath Common, and back."

"Sounds like a good plan," she agreed. "It's only half eight, and we could be at hers for about eleven. Usual arrangement?"

"Usual...?" Jack puzzled, scratching his head vacantly.

"Breakfast? Children? You know?" she laughed, pulling a face at his lack of thought. "Memory loss is the first sign of senility, you know."

"Oh," he grimaced, "brain's still in bed. Sorry. Just thinking about Val."

"I know," she muttered. "Nobody deserves that sort of treatment. That brother of yours makes me angry."

"He makes you angry?" Jack hissed, his eyes flashing. "Just the thought – the mere mention – makes my blood boil. I'd like to be having words with him right now."

"I think our Val will be able to handle matters herself," Jenny said, calmly. "We just need to be there for her and her delightful nippers, of course, whenever they need us. We've got plenty of space."

"Not heard from her since we moved?" he asked, as he began to prepare what he called his gourmet breakfast, made from ... porridge and fruit and tea, and ... more tea. "I mean, do you think she'll carry out her threat ... to leave?"

"If he doesn't do what's right," Jenny said slowly, "she will. She is usually very calm and forgiving, but you don't want to cross her. Takes a long time, but she will bite back."

"Anyway," Jack's five-minute warning began to sound in his head, "are the three of you ready for my fabulous gourmet offering? Five minutes."

"By the way," Jenny said, spoon rattling in here empty

dish.

"You mean there's another 'by the way' as well as how beautiful my porridge was?" he laughed.

"I don't think Mum knows about William," she said, ignoring his usual eulogy about his breakfast-making prowess. "So, if you'll pardon the pun, mum's the word."

-o-

"Oh, by the way, Mrs M," Jack started over lunch at the Plough, "have you heard anything from Val lately?"

Jenny's scimitar-like glance would have laid bare the flesh and bones of any mortal – other than Jack. He was mischievous in the extreme, and he knew which levers to pull to bring her emotional reaction to simmer. He was clever enough not to go too far, but his sense of humour and fun took him to the edge on many an occasion.

"As a matter of fact, I have," Jenny's mum replied as she tucked into her steak and kidney. "She didn't say as such, but I don't think all is right in that household. I'd been meaning to ask you both if either of your siblings had ... said anything? I wouldn't want her to bear any burdens on her own ... This steak and kidney's good."

"Can't do with it, missen," Jack said, a grimace of distaste edging his words. "It's offal."

Jenny threw a gentler but still warning glance at him, drawing a cheeky smile to his face ... the sort of smile which always softened her hard shell, and which told him he hadn't over-stepped her mark – yet.

"If there is a problem," Jenny added quickly, "I'm sure they will either sort it out for themselves, or they'll ask for guidance or support. Until that time, whatever is going on is their business, and it's not for us to interfere, eh, Jack?"

"Are we puddening?" he said, recognising Jenny's line in the sand, over which he would never step. He had a well-developed – if at times wicked – sense of humour, which had neither malice nor ill-thinking at its edge. He just loved the life he had now. Like-thinking, they felt there wasn't a problem they weren't able to sort out together, which was more than could be said for his brother and sister-in-law.

"I can't believe how well-behaved Jessie and Florence May are," Mrs McDermot said as she stroked Jessie's hair. "It's really so nice to be out with you all. It tends to get a bit tiring being at home, cooking for one."

"Then you must come and stay with us more often," Jack insisted. "We have plenty of space, and a large garage."

"Jack!" Jenny gasped. "You can't—"

"Jenny," her mum interrupted, "even I know when Jack's joking. You were joking, weren't you, Jack?"

"Of course I was," he replied, a huge grin agreeing with her. "But you can come anyway."

They all burst out laughing at his cheeky jokes, and Mrs McDermot let out a seriously contented sigh. She had not been this relaxed for a long while, and she didn't want the day to end.

"The hill we're approaching now," Jack said, driving slowly towards an unseen bend on his way to Kirkthorpe, "is called Marshall Hill, and it's one I remember to my cost. I first encountered it when I was eleven. I had just had my first and only full-size bike bought for passing my scholarship to t'Grammar School, and I was out with a couple of mates, on our way to Half Moon Lake.

"The bike was a Raleigh Palm Beach, had three Sturmy Archer gears, and felt like it had been built out of the turret of a Second World War tank. Anyway, I'd never been down any hill before, and found the bend at the bottom a bit hard to negotiate. I hit a patch of gravel, mi bike skidded, and I somersaulted – bike and all – over the fence at the bottom, into the field, narrowly missing the barbed wire, apparently."

"Oh, my God," Jenny gasped. "Did you hurt yourself?"

"Cut mi arm and leg, and grazed mi knees," he grinned, "but apart from that, just mi pride, I suppose."

"Short day, then," Jenny said, a look of concern etching her face, even though it was more than fifteen years before.

"Not really," he went on. "Front wheel was buckled, so I couldn't ride, but we did go on to the lake. Couldn't let mi mates down, you see. Any road, they'd have gone on without me, even if I'd turned round and walked home. They'd have thought I was soft. Couldn't have that."

Kirkthorpe was a pleasant little village which relied for its everyday life on its much larger close neighbour city, Wakefield, and its even closer neighbour, Normanton. Fortunately, a thrice-daily bus service linked the three, allowing the necessities of life to be brought in regularly.

Set in the Warmfield countryside with none of the problems dense urbanisation brings, Kirkthorpers had to endure a pretty, idyllic existence. Although ringed by mostly unseen pit headgear, and wracked by insignificant complaints about isolation and the noisy railway line just to its north, the inhabitants of this 'island' paradise luxuriated in the beauty of living in gloriously and relatively unspoiled countryside.

"The next time I came down here was to go fishing in the Half Moon Lake with mi mate Stuart Hodgson, when we were about fifteen," he continued, as they slowed past the end of Half Moon Lane. "We never caught owt, but it were real fun, walking around the end of the lake to the reeds on the inward curving stretch. We'd often talked about doing a bit of night fishing and camping by the water's edge, but we never had the bottle."

"Camping? You?" Jenny laughed.

"Aye," he answered, smiling at the thought. "It never appealed, really, except for once, when I were a nipper. About nine or ten I think we were. We once camped out on Harry Bowles' back lawn – big, big garden it were. Three of us threatened to stop in his little tent over night, but we thought better of it and went home to bed at about ten o'clock. My one and only foray into sleeping under canvass – except, that is, for spending an hour or so under the tent I made out of mi mam's wooden clothes horse and an old sheet, behind our wash house."

"This is lovely countryside," Mrs McDermot said as they rounded the corner just past Heath Hall and farm. "Never really explored around here, even with your dad, and you know how adventurous he was."

"Anyone fancy afternoon tea just round the next corner at the King's Arms?" Jack offered. "Never been in it myself, but folks say as it has many of its original features, and that it dates to medieval times. Only time I ever saw its outside was when we came to Heath Common Fair, most Easters."

"We came once to the fair," Jenny said, "but I didn't reckon much to it. Too noisy, too busy, and too … smelly. It would be lovely to have a cup of tea, though."

"You bought me a lovely lunch, Jack," Jenny's mum broke in, as they came to a halt, "so afternoon tea's on me."

"No, Mum," Jenny protested. "It's our treat today."

"I insist," her mother said firmly.

"Then, I'll have traditional afternoon tea, followed by—" Jack added quickly, making them laugh at the look of mock ecstasy on his face.

-o-

"That was a lovely day you gave my mum, Jack Ingles," Jenny sighed, kissing her husband as they sat down in their North Leeds palace once the children had been put to bed, "and one she won't forget."

"We must involve her more often," he answered, as he brought tea mugs and a steaming tea pot to her, "both to take out and for her to come here to stay. It can't be the best sort of existence when you're on your own, day in – day out, especially when one of your daughters lives only a cock stride away."

"You are such a good man, Jack," she said shuffling closer to him on their settee.

"And I don't cost anything, either," he said, a smile creasing his eye corners. "I'm good—"

"For nothing," she laughed, comfortable with his usual jokes.

"Well, my lovely," he whispered as he slid his arm around her shoulder, "just over a week and a half left of our wonderful summer holiday. For me it couldn't have been better, but I'm sorry we couldn't stretch to a week in the sun."

"Who needs foreign holidays, wasting money," she answered quickly, "when I have a husband who has given me all this? This is important to me, not galivanting off, giving money away to foreigners, and lining the pockets of fat-cat holiday magnates."

"We might be able to manage a few days away next year," he said, raising a promissory eyebrow.

"Scotland is where I'd like to go, actually," she replied, raising a hopeful smile in return. "Never been."

"Me neither," he added quickly. "See how the finances go, and then next year it might be the Ingles' world tour of Scotland. Sounds good to me seeing as I hate laying out in the sun, doing nothing. I couldn't think of anything more mind-numbing."

"You are funny, Jack Ingles," Jenny laughed. "I think I'm getting to know you, and then you throw in something totally unexpected. I thought you might have wanted to spend time in the South of France, for example, what with your French and all that."

"Instead, I'd rather go to Scotland, because I can speak English better than I can French," Jack said, "and I prefer Scots to Frogs. Rugged highlands have it over flat featureless vineyards any day."

He laid his head back on the settee and closed his eyes momentarily, as if reflecting on both the now and the when.

"Got to go to the bank in Moortown in the morning," he said, stifling a yawn. "Fancy a walk with Jess and Flo?"

"Course I do," she said without hesitation. "A morning out and a bit of exercise, after which we could perhaps have coffee and a cake in that new coffee shop on Street Lane?"

Jenny looked to her husband for agreement, but found his eyes still shut, and his breathing entering that state of relaxation just before sleep.

"Bedtime, my lovely," she said quietly, giving him a nudge, "or I'll be forced to tickle you."

"You wouldn't do that to a poor old man?" he yawned again. "Would you?"

"No, but you'll do instead," she laughed, touching his neck.

"All rayt. All rayt," he gasped, drawing his neck into his shoulders as far as he could so as not to be caught. He began to stretch and move slowly, ready to do his ablutions, but was, unfortunately, much too slow. Jenny leaped from her corner and made a swift beeline for the bathroom, clicking the door locked as she closed it, giggling at her own success.

"Too slow, old man," she shouted through the door. "You'll have to warm my side of the bed instead."

-o-

"I'm glad we came in by car," Jenny said, as they rounded Moortown Corner and were faced with the lengthy walk along Street Lane to the shops, past Talbot Road and opposite the Deer Park pub.

Not a million miles away from the official meteorological start of autumn, the sun still bore down out of a clear azure sky, although at this time of year the weather refused to acknowledge that it was still technically summer. Cloud would wander in, appearing as by magic, to spoil anyone's parade. Children were already playing out, finding spare pieces of ground upon which to indulge their favourite games. Knots of older ones cluttered the pavements and doorways, boredom already growing for want of anything that might tease the imagination.

"Nothing like when we were kids," Jack noticed, ever observant about human activity around him. "I used to climb trees and build swings and make throwing arrows when I was a nipper."

"Not the same today, I'm afraid, love," Jenny replied. "Brick and tarmac jungle here, unfortunately. We had Goosehill fields, don't forget."

"Yes, but we had to walk or cycle to get there from our concrete cage," he countered. "There's the most enormous public park just down the road that would swallow Haw Hill a hundred times over. Lack of imagination, that's the problem. They want it all laid out in their own back yard."

"Here's the coffee shop," Jenny said, changing the subject to make him dismount his hobby horse.

"OK," he said, a huge grin decorating his face. "A cup of tea and a piece of ... sponge cake for me, and—"

"Hello, Jack," a very familiar voice attacked him, turning him round quickly. "How are you?"

A slender, fair-haired woman stood before him, a restless little boy to hand.

"Lee?" he glowered, stiffening visibly. "What the bloody hell are you doing here?"

–o–

"Hit the Road, Jack" is the third book in the series about Jack Ingles. The first two books are:

Volume One: "Jack the Lad"
Volume Two: "Jack"

The fourth book will be called "Welcome Back, Jack" and it will be released towards the end of 2017.

Author – Frank English

Born in 1946 in the West Riding of Yorkshire's coal fields around Wakefield, he attended grammar school, where he enjoyed sport rather more than academic work. After three years at teacher training college in Leeds, he became a teacher in 1967. He spent a lot of time during his teaching career entertaining children of all ages, a large part of which was through telling stories, and encouraging them to escape into a world of imagination and wonder. Some of his most disturbed youngsters he found to be very talented poets, for example. He has always had a wicked sense of humour, which has blossomed only during the time he has spent with his wife, Denise. This sense of humour also allowed many youngsters to survive often difficult and brutalising home environments.

Eleven years ago he retired after forty years working in

schools with young people who had significantly disrupted lives because of behaviour disorders and poor social adjustment, generally brought about through circumstances beyond their control. At the same time as moving from leafy lane suburban middle class school teaching in Leeds to residential schooling for emotional and behavioural disturbance in the early 1990s, changed family circumstance provided the spur to achieve ambitions. Supported by his wife, Denise, he achieved a Master's degree in his mid-forties and a PhD at the age of fifty-six, because he had always wanted to do so.

Now enjoying glorious retirement, he spends as much time as life will allow writing, reading and travelling.